BEER, FIGHTING AND TABS

Published by the Penguin Group
27 Wrights Lane, London W8 5TZ, England
Viking Penguin Inc., 40 West 23rd Street, New York,
New York 10010, USA
Penguin Books Australia Ltd, Ringwood, Victoria,
Australia
Penguin Books Canada Ltd, 2801 John Street, Markham,
Ontario, Canada L3R 1B4
Penguin Books (NZ) Ltd, 182-190 Wairau Road,
Auckland 10, New Zealand

Penguin Books Ltd, Registered Offices: Harmondsworth,
Middlesex, England

First published 1988
10 9 8 7 6 5 4 3 2 1

Designed by Giant
Photography by Derek Ridgers
Extra photography by Clint Eley

Special thanks to Fiona Reilly (Missy Wissy), Adam, Kath and Daphne
Athanassiou and friends, Fluck and Law, Dave 'Naughty Puppy'
Cummings, Gerry, Maria, Debra, Roz and Angela (The Doynton Street
Mob), Mark Rollinson, Wesley Alden, Sarah Howling…
…oh yeah – and Jonathan Woss.

Filmset by Rowland Phototypesetting Ltd, Bury St Edmunds,
Suffolk

Made and printed in Great Britain by
Richard Clay Ltd, Bungay, Suffolk

Ace Photo Agency 16, 17, 25, 52, 81;   Allsport 9, 18/19;   Andes Press Agency 25;   Barnaby's Picture
Library 37, 53;   BBC Hulton Picture Library 19;   Camera Press 7, 33, 41, 63, 78, 79;   Bruce Coleman
11;   Sally and Richard Greenhill 7;   The Image Bank 53, 80;   Keystone Collection 10, 41, 52/53,
53;   London Features International 34, 36, 41, 63, 78, 79;   Mansell Collection 27;   Photographers'
Library 81;   Pictor International 81;   Popperfoto 7;   Sporting Pictures 52;   Syndication International
70;   Bob Thomas 41;   Reg Wilson 25.

Hi, readers,

English, phew, what a language, fascinating, or what, eh? In the words of the great linguist Professor P.B.J. Leavis: 'I am always fascinated by the multifarious variations of dialect and syntax – the rich tapestry of colloquialisms, the warp and weft of words within this, our Sceptred Isle.'

Others have said, 'Bollocks!', notably Loadsamoney, Professor of 'I Don't Mind Speaking My Mind', at the University of Life (expelled 1974-8).

Anyway here's a handy cut-out 'n' lose guide to some of the phrases you may encounter on your travels around this book.

love Sir Peter Penguin, XXX

PPPPS, Buy my biscuits.

ENGLISH	STAVROS	LOADS
Cigarettes	Coughin' Jimmy Nails	'Avannah cigar, mate
Match	Arse v. Spurs	Gold Dunhill lighte (fill 'er up, 2 gallon of 4-star, and you can shove your free glasses up your arse
Drink	Large Brand and Nesquik	Pint of champagne
Soft drink	Tap wart' (with bubs)	Heineken
Toilets	Genital-man's	Bog-hole
Bilious attack	Chund'	Pavement pizza
Car	Not applicable (I'm got a Skoda)	Roadshagger
Passenger	Her inside the car	Seat cover
Accident	Tradge'	New motor
Ambulance	ecnalubmA	Burn–up time
Hospital	Close down	Nurseville
Unemployed	Up the 'ole King Cole	Not applicable
DHSS	Depart' of Elfs and SS Nazi barsts'	Somewhere to go for a really good laugh
Brain	Michael Caine	Nut
Private parts	My little Lester Piggs	Joy dispenser
Eyes	Morecombe & Wise	Minces
French-kiss	Sexy tongue munch	Hors d'oeuvres

GGERALL

kfast (& dinner,
a)

r face, my arse

nk beer, me

you calling me a
, or what?

users

ooaaarghhh

tray

spilt ma pint?

ile home

kend retreat

ne bastard home

vt

dispenser

k

you trying to
my tab?

USEFUL PHRASES

ENGLISH	**How fantastic! I've won two free tickets for tonight's ballet at the Theatre Royal.**
STAVROS	Lor' luv a **Swan Lake!** We's won a couple of ticks' for tonight's poncy la-di-da, tu-tu, Russian, nancy-boy peeps defect over the wall on tiptoe or what.
LOADS	**Free** tickets?!? **SHUT YOUR MOUTH!**
BUGGERALL	Way, ay, me luck's in. Two tickets for a free puff-bashin' session up at the Theatre Royal the neet.
ENGLISH	**My, what a lovely kitchen you have here, Dolores.**
STAVROS	Blimey, is a brand spanky tickety-shiny-boo kitch wiv' all the mod pros and cons tha' yous got, innit?
LOADS	You what? Only one bleedin' microwave? I got TEN an' they're all tellies an' all, probly.
BUGGERALL	Ay, pet, it's alreet this kitchen but the sink's a bit high, so there's quite a lot of piss on yer floor now.
ENGLISH	**Excuse me, aren't you Penelope Keith?**
STAVROS	Blimey, Penelope Keith, innit? You is the spitting image of her-inside-the-doors, except tha' she's little, portly an' Greek.
LOADS	Oy! Ain't you that ugly ponce off of **The Good Life**. I always preferred the other bird on it, meself, lovely bum.
BUGGERALL	Hoo there, pet, did you just drop one or was it me? Awww! That's a real Brussel sprouter! Fancy a fight?

STAVGAG

WHOOPS!

♪ DEE-DING, DIDDLEY-DING, DIDDLE-DIDDLE-DING. ♫

WHEN IS COME TO SPILLAGES, JUS' CALL ME **ABZORBA THE GREEK!**

MY MOUSTACHE A PICTORIAL HIST',
by Moustavroche

I'm wonder if you happ' to note the little hairy thing meanderin' lovingly betwix' my upper lip and my conk. That's right, my moust'. As every blinkin' bloke worth his sort of pepper is know, a moust is a must for the mod male about Hackney.

First, is a sign of viril. The ladies is love to maker the love-make sexy snog with a hairy lip-slug nestin' in their nosts'. Top mods is say, 'Give me a hairy-face' man like Stav any day rather than one with the face like a baby's bum, innit?'

Second, if you's go billiard-balled as a coot, you can always train you moustache up the side of you face and over the top of you head, to meet in a nice centre part'. Mind you, some top mods is also find bald viril, and they have been heard to say, 'Give me a hairy-face' man with a head like a baby's bum any day of the week, please.'

Third, is come in pretty blood' use as a fork and spoon. Just dip it in you food, and suck it off the ends. Or you can leave it there in storage for the long dark wint' nights, when, if you can grow it long enough, you can also use it as ear muffs and a scarf.

Fourth, with a 'tache you can change you appearance at will. To show you what I mean, here are some pics showing the development of my hirsute appendage.

The pencil moustache.

The handle-bar moustache.

The ~~Adolf Hitler~~ Charlie Chaplin look.

The Salvador Dali look.

The Jimmy Hill'tache of the day look.

Me today with the Solidarnosc look.

Five weeks old, with the five-year-plan 'Josef Stalin' look.

The Edwardian Teddy-boy look.

Actually this wasn't a moustache. I'd just eaten a squirrel.

Other fame' peeps who is sport the moustavros look

The Queen Mum.

Telly Savalas.

Telly Woges.

Sunday Snort

IT'S A DOUBLE STAV-TRICK!

Spurs salute superb six-shooter Stav, as the moustachioed maestro sinks Gunners.

WEMBLEY has never seen a cup final like it. Right from the start the Arsenal defence was torn apart by Spurs' middle-aged wonderboy, Stavros. Six goals in as many minutes from silky Stav put paid to Arsenal's cup aspirations. After the final whistle had blown and the cup was held aloft by the jubilant Spurs players, only Bobby Robson thought Arsenal were still in with a chance.

After their six-goal slamming, Arsenal lose not only the FA cup but also, by an ironic twist of fate, their place in the League, as any team losing a Wembley final by six goals is automatically relegated to the Vauxhall Opel Conference, permanently. With no hope of ever returning to the League, the Arse-

Bubble's Double means Double Trouble

nal board has decided to disband the club and sell Highbury Stadium to a leading fast-food consortium. The famous old ground will then be turned into a huge 50,000-seater 'Kentucky Fried Kebab' eating house. 'We intend to put every small Greek kebab shop in London out of business,' said their chairman, Sir Ron Bastard.

Arsenal lose not onl
but also, by an ironi
their place in the l
also, by an iron
the
Wem
s dec
sel
ading
amou
ned i
seater Kentuc
eating house.
every small G
London out of l
chairman, Sir
goals is autom
the Vauxhal
permanently
returning to
the club an
dium to a le
tium. The f
then be tur
seater 'K
eating ho
every sm
London o
chairma
Arsenal
but also
their pl
team lo
goals is
the V
perma
retur
nal b

The 'Dukakis' Rough Guide to Hackney

The guide books 'Dukakis', both practical and full of informations, are among the best of the Greek quality guides. The authors of the guides 'Dukakis' have try to summary the most import' informations relate to hist' folklaw and modern cultch' and tourist life, include toilet facils'.

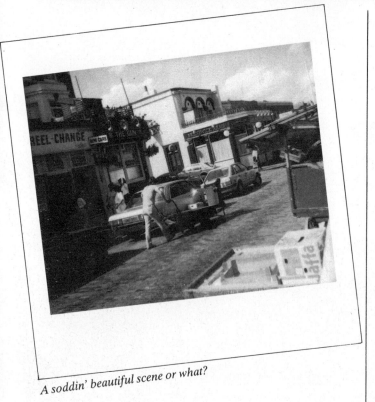

A soddin' beautiful scene or what?

THE GUIDE BOOKS 'DUKAKIS' WELCOME YOU IN HACKNEY AND WISH YOU A PLEASANT HOLIDAYS.

Hackney, O Hackney! The very word is conjure up a beautiful spot! This charm' and harmonious region is sometimes note' as The Jewel in The Crowd. The cap' town of the borough, partake of Bethnals Green in the southern aspect, Dalston tenuously clutch' her Western shores, and lovely Clapton in the North, truly it is a dump.

Don't miss the populous and bustling.

Town centre with her colourful shops and friendly artisans in the costumes unique to this colloquial and historic areas. Like the happy Wheel-Clampers who is go about their ancient trade, a-whistling in their distinct' Denver Shoes. Forget-me-not on your travels.

SIGHTS OF THE REGION

Be sure to oversee the renowned caves and craters of Morning Lane as is sweep majest' towards the glorious and impressive Eastway, beyond which is lie the celebrashe' Wick of Hackney. Old Father Mare Street, roll' lugubriously past the splendid architecture of the Town Hall and Mr Pepys Over-21 Bar, where time has stood still for years, ever since the clock is stop.

Also the quiet and sleepy Narrow way, which can be understood to meander back and forth among distraught clothing shops and the characteristic sellers of hip, hop, 'house', rap-n-reggae and the 'et cetera'. Also the antique ruins of the many charming housing estates, and the dramatic rock formashe' of the building sights stand' mute witness to centuries of sedate labour.

INTERESTING PLACES FOR SWIMMING

The deep blue waters of the Clapton baths, have lure' poets and artists over many years. Was it not W. H. Auden who is say, 'Excuse me, I think that's my towel'? Also the baths at Hoxton who are fame for their chlorine-rich aqua, there.

See also the Ancient Spa, situate' on Kingsland Road, one of the most fame' spas in this part of North East London. Where you can make the purchase of eye-drops for after you' swim.

One of the many charm' sights to be seen in the travel agent's window on Mare Street.

ANCIENT MONUMENTS

There are a multitude of Castles in Hackney. The Windsor Castle on Upper Clapton Road, the Dublin Castle on Cambridge Heath Road, and the romantic ruins of the Edinburgh Castle on Wick Road, which is never recover from New Year's Eve 1987.

Hackney is also boast over fifty Public Toilets, though why anyone is want to boast about toilets is beyond me.

Many fine architectures abound. Notably to this fact, are the Byzantine pillarage system and Corinthian in design cornice. Abound.

FLORA AND FAUNA

The most congenital place to spy the Flora is in Supermarket Tesco on The Ancient and historic market of Well Street. Here also can be found the home of the Stork. And many characteristic local dishes, include the Leslie Crowther, stand mute witness to centuries of bad advertise'.

But indeed there are many indignant wildlifes in Hackney. And a rich variety of glorious and rampant vegetables. Such examples as trees, and grass. And many flowers of different colours. From the rainbow, the popular place to see flowers is in the flower shop.

Rats.

O, Hackney! Yes, you have much creatures among the landscapes, lovely lady.

DOG
Most common of the idiomatic and appropiate animals of the region, are the many and various dogs. All types are represent, from the humble Collie to the proud Mastiff with it's distinctive mange. Maybe if Lady Luck is bounty', you may even see an unprecedent' Cairn Terrier, or a Pit Bull Terrier, with it's idiosincratic testicles. But be awary of danger, a great many of these mentioned afore dogs might care to bite you legs off.

CAT
In Hackney can be found a multitude of cats (feline), some kept as pets inside the home, some living wildly in herds. All types are reprehensible. With the cats also can be discover' another example of characteristic wild life, the charming flea.

Pigeon.

PIGEON
Sometimes this Plebeian of the air is refer' to as a flying rat.

RAT
Sometimes refer' to as a crawling pigeon.

LAD
Beware this vicious and unpredict' beast. With heady intoxicashe'. Famille' mating cry of Woooooargh!

FESTIVALS AND CULTURAL EVENTS
Watch out for the Festival of Masks, outside the Midland Bank, followed by the Carnival of the Wailing Sirens.

Join in the Old MacDonald 'Hadda' Ritual, ee-i-ee-i-oh! And make a wish as you discard you own big 'MacCarton' in the street outside the shrine of Ronald of the Golden Arches on the Narrow Way.

Folk Dancing – there are many clubs down along the Hakcney Road, where can be seen folk dancing of a weekend, include' the Dance of the Handbags, the tradish' male dance 'Are you looking at my bird?', and not to be missed is plate-smashing, glass-smashing, window-smashing. And the Parade of the Ambulances.

PLASTERING MADE EASY

A step-by-step guide to plastering in an easy way. By me, Loadsamoney.

TOOLS OF THE TRADE:

a) Radio, broken (volume control stuck on extra loud).
b) Newspaper (*Sun*).
c) Bum–revealing trousers.
d) Fags.
e) Slave (Lance).

STEP 1: THE QUOTE, OR 'SUCK JOB'

The first thing you will need to do when looking at any job is suck your breath in between your teeth while shaking your head.

These are some of the technical terms you will need at this most crucial stage of the job:

a) Cost ya.
b) Damp course.
c) Cash.
d) Any danger of a cup of tea?

STEP 2: UPPING THE QUOTE

The night before starting the job you should always contact the client and up your quote. It is a simple technique, but you'll be pleasantly surprised by the results.

Useful things to remember when upping your quote are:

a) Materials.
b) Labour.
c) Rolex.
d) Holiday in the Bahamas.

STEP 3: GETTING STARTED

STEP 4: USING CLIENT'S PHONE

It is always best to use the client's phone whenever possible, especially when ordering up supplies such as lager and dinner.

STEP 5: THE DIRTY JOKE

STEP 6: OFFERING SUGGESTIONS TO PASSING LADIES

Some useful phrases:
a) Waaaaoooorgh.
b) Yaaaaaaah.
c) Ooo–Oooo–Ooo–Waaah.

STEP 7: ART

Look at all these teabags, cups and fag-ends and that. They'd pay a few bob for that lot down the Tate Gallery, probly.

STEP 8: FARTING

The good thing about dropping one is that Lance always thinks it's him.
Types of fart you may like to try:
a) Eggy.
b) The Brussel Sprout.
c) The SBV
d) The Fog-Horn.
e) The Cushion Creeper.
f) The Derek Nimmo.
g) The Chernobly (proper supervision advised).

STEP 9: DINNER

Lance has worked particularly hard today, so I bought him a nice big dinner – a spud.

STEP 10: SANDING DOWN

Investing the client's money on the 3.15 at Sandown.

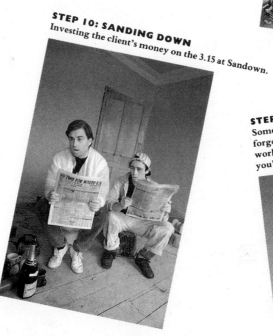

STEP 11: THE DUMP

Some days, due to lack of materials (because you forgot to order them, probly), you can't do any work. So it's important to let the customer know you've been there. Foul the toilet.

STEP 12: UMMM . . .

STEP 13: THAT'LL DO FOR TODAY

Sick Page

I had to go into hospital last week. Private, natch. 5-star. I was in me own exclusive luxury penthouse ward – four tellies, cash-point, full a la carte menu and wine list, mink trimmed bed-pan, the lot. It was so bleeding palatial that I reckon I'll go there for me holidays next year. Not that it was all, you know, feet up and pissing about and that. No, I was in for some highly complex and intricate micro-surgery, as it goes. One little slip and it could have spelt disaster for the patient, in this case, namely, yours truly, me, i.e. Loadsamoney, etc. So they've gone and got in the world's leading specialist – a pioneer in the field of blonde highlight surgery. And just about the only geezer in the civilised universe who could cater to my very specific hairstyling requirements. He done a great job and all. In fact I was so be-holden up to him, that I done him a favour back. Yeah, I've sent him a couple of tickets for our 'Biggest Builder's Arse of the Year' competition down my club next week. I reckon he'd like that, probly.

All them nurses they got down there, phwoar! They love having me in for 'treatment', cause I'm such a great laugh, you know, jokes and that. And, like, of course, them bein' nurses they're always dying for it aren't they? Yeah, and who am I to stand in the way of the modern woman's needs? Waargh!

I remember I thought about becoming a doctor meself, once, as it goes. You know, examining up all them birds with me stethoscope. Only it turned out that me handwriting was too good for Medical College. And anyway them doctors and that don't get paid cash in hand, do they? No. I mean, when was the last time you saw the Sturgeon General waving about an even halfway decent-sized wad? Exactly! I rest my case…Nurse! NURSE! It's time for us to take each other's temperatures again. Yaaaargh!!

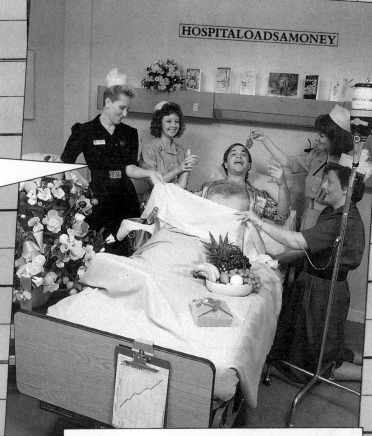

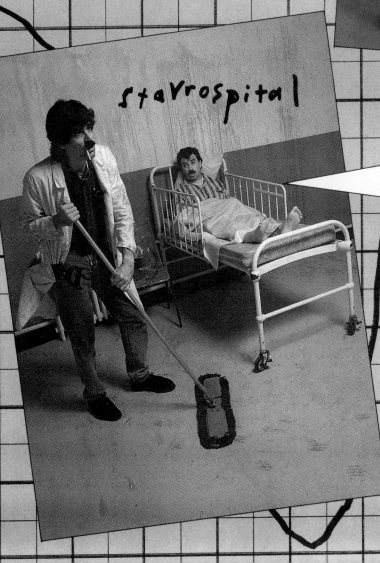

One morn' a couple of weeks ago, old Postman Pete is pop the Royal Mail through my box as usual and I'm have a quiet sift through it innit? Well, one of the letts is a real bolt-upright wild shocker from out the blue yond'. You could have knocked me out with a featherweight. Tha's right it was my long await hosp' appoint' for my operashe'. Blimey is so long ago when I'm first try for this appoint', tha' the bloody Dinosaurs was still gambolling about down the Bethnal Greens Road, innit? Yeah, thanks to the bloody Ironing Lady, Her Inside Number Ten, the poor old Nash' Health Serve' is certainly suffer from a very severe under-the-fund. They's even ask me to bring my own needle and thread with me when I'm come in for surge'!

The bloke with me tha' you can see in the photo' is call Alf Todgington. Alf was inish' taken on as a domestic orderly, but because of back-cuts and short-staffages, he was recently been ask' to try his hand at the odd heart-bypass operashe'. According to Alf, there is actually very little to choose between the two jobs, but when push is become shove, he is slightly prefer his work with mop and bucket over his skills with the scalp', innit? Mind you, as he is pain-fully point out, is purely a matter of personal opin', and some peeps might well fave' the challenge of maje' heart surgery.

I'm learn quite a lot too while I was 'inside.' Mainly about aneasthatizashe'. Well I'm bloody had to, innit? Yeah, the aneasth-bloke is not flippin' turn up to knock me out for the countdown during my op, so I'm had to do it myself. Actually I'm not get the amounts quite right and I'm wake up halfway through on the operate' tabe', surround by a team of masked medicos. Luckily my innards was such a horrible fright' sight – a big gory mess of blood kidneys, liver and bacon, lungs and stringy bits, that I'm out-black again straightaway, pronto. So the operashe' is evench' go fairly swimmily. In fact the 'what's up' Doc is say that after a brief period of convalesce' I'll be abe' to take the plaster off my hand and no-one will ever even know I'm had a wart there in the first place.

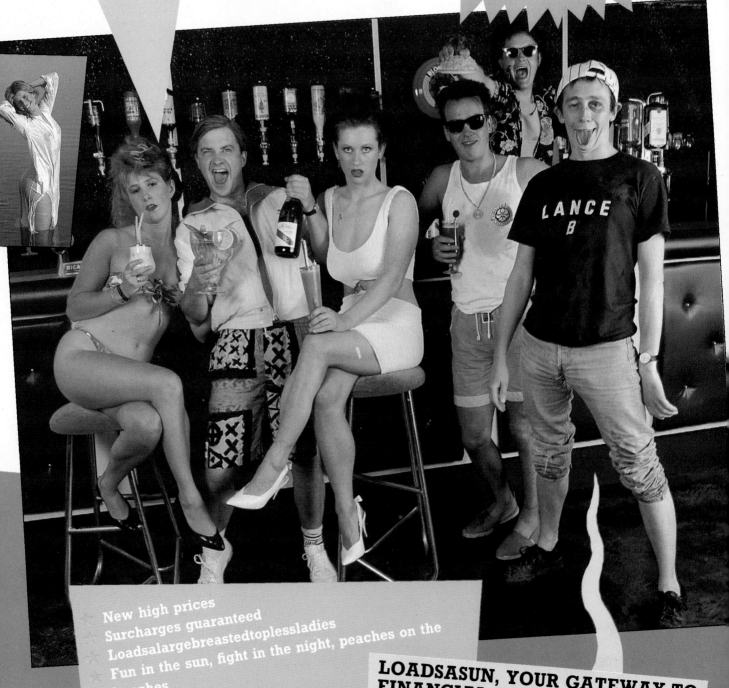

LOADSASUN HOLIDAYS

INVITE YOU TO ENJOY THE PLEASURES OF

CLUB WAD

- New high prices
- Surcharges guaranteed
- Loadsalargebreastedtoplessladies
- Fun in the sun, fight in the night, peaches on the beaches
- No kids
- Well-hung gliding
- Nipple with your tipple
- Topless shoe-cleaning service

LOADSASUN, YOUR GATEWAY TO FINANCIAL RUIN

Quality, reliability and value, just three of the things we won't bother you with on your Loadsasun Holiday of a lifetime at one of our **CLUB WAD** resorts.

THE LOADSASUN PRICE PROMISE

While other companies simply talk about it, we **GUARANTEE** higher prices. Yes, with Loadsasun you get extra all the way. **EXTRA** surcharges. **EXTRA** long waits at airports. **EXTRA** people sharing your room. Plus a whole range of what we in the biz call **HIDDEN EXTRAS**. Like airport tax, food tax, hidden extra people in the room tax, sun tax, tax tax . . . the list is endless!

LET US TAKE CARE OF YOU

Luggage problems? Not with **LOADSASUN** because once you leave Gatwick you'll never see it again.

Confused by foreign exchange rates? Not any more. With **LOADSASUN'S** unique foreign exchange rate system it's child's play.

For instance for **ONE POUND**, you get, **ONE LIRA**. Or perhaps you're going to Greece. Then for **ONE POUND**, we'll give you, **ONE DRACHMA**. And so on. What could be simpler?

EXPENSIVE HOTELS

LOADSASUN only books you into the most expensive hotels in the most expensive resorts, but don't worry: expensive doesn't necessarily mean better.

So, without more ado, it's over to our chairman, Mr Loadsamoney, to fill you in on the details.

There are many tropical beaches on the Seychelles.

THE SEYCHELLES

God knows where the Seychelles are. He ought to – he put 'em there, probly. But it's hot and abroad, so it's ideal for a holiday. Clear turquoise seas, coral reefs and that, means you got a kaleidoscope of the world's most beautiful and rare fish swarming up all over the place. So be sure to pack your spear-gun.

HOTEL BRIANNE CLOEUFFE

Mahe Island has some of the world's most unspoilt beaches, but don't let that put you off because the Hotel Brianne Cloeuffe is miles away from them, and that's where you'll be staying. It's truly one of the world's most spoilt hotels, where you can get pissed up all day long without any danger of getting sand up your thong.

FACILITIES
Plenty of bogs. Twenty-four-hour happy hour. Dangerous watersports. Disco. Graveyard.

BAR RATING *
TOPLESS BEACH RATING ***
**ANNOYING FOREIGNER RATING **

PRICES (exclusive of VAT and any other extras we can think of)

1 WEEK	£1,254.98
2 WEEKS	£3,554.76
3 WEEKS	£22,244.87

Exciting night-life in old Bangkok.

BANGKOK

Lives up to its name, *waaaargh.* Apparently there's some lovely old buildings and temples. Well, bollocks to that. I mean, we all know why people come here – not that I've ever paid for it in my life. **THEY PAY ME.**

HOTEL THAI MI UPP

The Hotel Thai Mi Upp offers a wide range of services for the modern traveller. Vibrating beds (batteries not supplied), 'interesting' videos (remember to take your Rolex off), ping-pong and also table tennis. There's lots of people available to give you a hand, *mega-waaaargh!* So there's plenty of opportunities to get baby oil up your thong.

FACILITIES
Twenty-four-hour clinic
DANGEROUS DISEASE RATING •••••••••••••••••••••••••

PRICES

1 WEEK	£2,333.33
2 WEEKS	£5,555.55
3 WEEKS	FORGET IT, MATE. NO ONE'S EVER LASTED THREE WEEKS

On the piste.

ST MORITZ

Miles and miles of sandy beaches. Well, snowy mountains. Specially for the lover of big peaks, know what I mean? Pack your snorkel for the jacuzzi.

HÔTEL EDDIE LE EAGLE

You'll meet a better class of bird at the Hôtel Eddie Le Eagle. You know why they call them the jet-set, don't you? Yeah, because they don't half go. And if you didn't manage to join the mile-high club on the way over, have a go off of the ski-jump. But mind you don't get a load of snow up your thong. *Brrrr!*

FACILITIES
Ski-rumpo. Splints. Cable car to transport your wad up the mountain. Hot'n'runny Swiss cheese for you to get your fork into if you fancy a fondue. Swiss banking (for those poor bastards that can't get hold of any birds).

CELEBRITY BIRD RATING •••••••••••••••
INTERNATIONAL FINANCE RATING •••••••••••••••••••••••••
BEACH RATING *

PRICES

1 WEEK	£28,000,000.99
2 WEEKS	A SECURICOR VAN FULL OF GOLD BULLION SHOULD COVER IT
3 WEEKS	YOU'RE JOKING

Helicopter bombing raid, somewhere over Benidorm.

BENIDORM

Too full of Club 18–30 wankers who are only after one thing: beer and birds. I don't do holidays there, but you can hire a helicopter and go on bombing missions (JULY AND AUGUST ONLY).

HOTEL EL TEL

A favourite target for our customers is the Hotel El Tel on the Costa Buggerall. Feel free to ask your friendly pilot José to swoop in low and rescue up any birds you might fancy. But watch out for shrapnel up your thong.

FACILITIES
Easily spotted from the sky. Plenty of other hotels nearby in case you miss. Shoddy construction – falls down a treat.

COMBAT RATING ***
MORON RATING **

CHOPPER RENTAL PRICES

1 BOMBING MISSION	£1,223.76
2 BOMBING MISSIONS	£2,643.00
3 BOMBING MISSIONS	WE HAVEN'T MADE THIS ONE UP YET

(Special nuclear option to be introduced next year. See press for details.)

Up the Arse!

The thing that I'm look forward to most every week is going up the Arse with Her Inside the Doors. We's a right bloody pair of Gooners, innit? Yeah, every Saturday we is shout our guts out from the north face of Highbury. Why? I ask you hear. Because they is flippin' brilliant, thas why, you stupid bast'. Espesh' since the saviour is return to On Highbury. I'm not mean John 'Lord' Lukic, the goal saviour, no. I'm talk about George 'Billy' Graham. He who was cast down into the lion's den down in dark satanic Millwall, only to survive the Wildness and come back a second time.

Arse Past

As everybodypeeps is know, the Arse is one of the oldest and most disting' teams in the world of sock'. They cupboard is so full of trophes past and pres' that they is probably need to buy a new one soon. They is consistently been the best team ever since before time immemorial. Only the other day I was look through my 'crapbook and lo and behind some other stuff I'm find a very old match report. Is from 1386.

The new-look Arse.

The Caunterbury Tymes

THE FOOTBALLE COURESPONDAUNTES TALE

Whan that Arsnill with hir gooles soote
The teame of Spures hath perced to the roote,
And alle the Gooneres dronk on stronge licour
Have chyred the score whych blossommed as a flour;
5   So priketh hem Tennents in hir corages
Thanne longen fannes to goon rampages,
Alas, to see folk as they capyre and cavorte,
Tis a sadde day for Brytyshe sporte.

From tavernes and from every shires ende
10   Of Engelonde to Highbury they wende,
And the voices of the fannes did maken melodye,
For yonge and olde do sorely love a Londoun derbye.
The skye was clere azur, and a hotte sonne
Did shyne as Arsnill hath onto the pytche yronne,
15   A rorre wente up so loud it strucke me deffe
As the whyslle was sootely sounded by the reffe.
A SENTYRE FORWARD ther was, and that a worthy man.
That fro the happye tyme he first bigan
To playye, he loved to scor the goole,
20   And so he tooke the balle withotte more rigmaroole.
Fro Spures he playd, and spures he wonne
As down the winge he swift yronne
Lyk Zephirus he flew past alle defensse
And alle the Gooners in the crowd becaym qyt tensse
25   The balle lypte from his foote, the nette to seke,
But clymbed too hye, and as a parotte he was seeke.
Fro that momente to the ende it was The Arsnill's gayme
But one manne from the matche deseverves fayme,
A WYNGERRE RYTE ther was, of Arsnill teyme
30   So faste he was a blure, so it wolde seyme,
For no man of Spures colde holde hem harde,
And two tymes ther goollye kaught he was off garde.
A third tym he tryde but hit the wood,
A trifficke littel stryker this, the ladde donne good.
35   Two gooles to non then for The Arsnill was the final scorre,
And if not fro waystinge tyme by Spures ther wolde be morre.
At ende of day the Arsnill was the betterre teyme,
With play lyk this, to ther playerres it must seyme
Lyk horses to the charyot of the moon they hitche.
40   A good days sporte, then, spoyled by vylnesse off the pitche.

3   A Goonere is believed to be a follower of Arsnill,
5   They are encouraged by strong ale into acts of bravery,
6   Then fans desire to go on the rampage.
21   Some confusion here between the team of Spures and the practice of awarding spurs (spures) to those who have done well.
23   Zephirus: god of the wind.

Good Arse

'There's peeps on the pitch, they think it's all over! Radford! George! It is now!!' So say the legend' commentate as Charlie George is struck home the win goal in the '71 Cup Fine' to complete the immort' dub'. Oh, happy days! Is etch-a-sketch into my Gordon Memory-Banks. This seas', however, I'm don' think they is gonna do the dub' again. NO! THEY IS GONNA DO THE TRIP', INNIT?

This is the legend' Arse Cup win team of 1912. As you can see, is the first team to be made up with 100% of my relashe'.

The Arse is unstoppable. You only got to look at the competishe to see tha's patently pendin' obvious. So here's my unbias' quick-as-a-glance-easy-look-guide to the so-called teams in the first divish'.

LIVER'N'BACONPOOL
Last seas' they is turn the first divish' into a one-team horse. Blimey, they is gonna look like the back end of a pantomime horse when the Gunners is finish with them this year.

ERIC HEFFERTON
Another team of Scouse, but this lot's had they gory, gory days a couple of years ago, and I'm don' see Howard 'Felicity' Kendall gettin' them to the top this year. Especially as he don' manage them no more.

MANCHESTER GOODNIGHTPEEPS (not to be confuse' with Manchester Shit)
They is still crap even though they is dump old Major Ron 'Donkey-face' Atkinson for Alex Fergie Big-bum. Mighty-Arse is gonna wipe the floor with them, innit?

NUKE-ARSE
The Jord' lads have been joined by that nut from Brazil, Miriamstoppardinha. But, I'm afraid, to me is a case of Tyne, Gentlemens, please!

NOTTABLOODYHOPE FOREST
Not a bloody lot for me to say about this bunch, unlike they boss, Lord Byron Cluff, who is all goal-mouth and no trousers, innit?

MILLDEW
A new entry in the charts, renown' for their fast, attacking footer and their fast, attacking fans. With all the violins on the terraces is a terrib' advert for our nash game. And anyway the Arse is gonna slaughter them.

LUTON LORRAINELANKYLEGS-CHASEBAST TOWN
Don' mention they beat the Arse in the Litterbugs cup. I SAID DON' MENSH'!!!!!!!!

TOTTINGHAM HOTPIES (THE COCKROACHES)
Lastly and leastly the lily-white crap. Since they bin took over by Terry 'The Wad' Vegetables they is gone from bad to basts. I'm think they is shortly due to follow the Chels', who is been relegate to the Flower Show, along with Pomp and Circumstance and poor old Elton, who is forced to sell all his clothes and his wigs in order to pay the rent.

HURRAH FOR HARRY!

Britain's top funny man, Harry 'That's showbiz, peeps!' Enfield, CBE, returns to our screens this week with a new series of *Laughter Eight with Harry*. Our light entertainment correspondent, Wills Windsor, tracked Harry down to his luxury country retreat and chemical research centre in rural Berkshire to ask him about his twenty years at the top of the comedy tree.

I found Harry – or Sir Harry, as some of his friends now wickedly dub him (and it can surely only be a matter of time) – reclining on a Louis Quatorze chaise-longue in his comfortable, unpretentious sitting-room. With a genial wave of his hand, Harry turned to his heavily armed body guard and said, 'I am one of Britain's best loved entertainers. Now get out.'

He gave a little laugh and, turning on the ingratiating smile that has become his trademark, asked me sincerely, 'Who did you say you were again?'

That's the thing about lovable Harry – he just can't stop joking.

But what did he think of those older comedians, like Lord Tarbuck of Butlin's, who maintain that these middle-aged comedians just aren't funny?

'Well,' said Harry, lighting a cigar, 'I think they have to admit that I'm something of an exception, don't they?'

Looking around at the plush surroundings, I reflected that he'd come a long way since those early days on the BBC, after his brief flirtation with Channel 4. (Whatever happened to Channel 4?)

People still remember his first BBC series, the fast 'n' furious sketch show *Rifling Around with Enfield*, primarily because it's been repeated regularly ever since. The show was designed (as were all BBC sketch shows at the time) to look exactly like *Not the Nine O'Clock News*, which had finished nearly ten years earlier.

'It was a wonderfully marvellous time, dear boy. So exciting. A great team.'

Did he still see any of the other 'Riflers', as they were known, I asked – people like Charlie Higson and Paul 'Whitey' Whitehouse?

'Oh, were they in it?' he replied, reaching for another bottle of champagne.

I agreed that it must be difficult remembering all the excellent team of support actors, especially as it was the custom at the time to quietly drop anyone who looked like they might upstage the star.

In 1992, the year of the television personalities' strike, he won the *TV Times* award for Television Personality of the Year and, in his controversial acceptance speech to nobody, said, 'Quite honestly, I didn't notice the picket line was there.'

Later that year, during the run-up to the general election, Harry campaigned vigorously against the policies of the Conservative government, which his speech-writers saw as 'divisive, damaging and, er, divisive'.

'Those were heady days,' said Harry. 'I've always held firm political convictions. I don't agree with those people who say you shouldn't mix politics and entertainment.'

Shortly afterwards he was awarded the CBE by President-designate Carol Thatcher and made several well-known ads for the Conservative Party, publicizing the privatization of capital punishment. His family appeal was further enhanced when he was appointed the new Wogan in 1993 (Terry being required to forfeit his surname along with his salary).

'Terry was a dear, dear friend, and a real pro. I often wonder what happened to him.'

It was as Harry Wogan that he hosted the Norman Vaughan Eightieth Birthday tribute when, together with Lord Daltrey of Trout and Dame John Inman, he performed that now legendary version of the old Who classic 'My Generation' and, to tumultuous applause, rounded off the evening by tap-dancing with Dusty Bin.

'Dear, dear Dusty. A real friend and a dear pro. Such a shame about the sex scandal.'

In 1999 he was voted king of the chat shows following five years of the successful *Get Oily with Harry*. I asked him which he preferred to do – chat shows or comedy?

'It depends on the fee,' quipped the king, in a flash.

Harry's not reluctant to talk about his private life and declares himself blissfully content with his sixteen-year-old wife of over four weeks who, like his previous eight wives, had appeared on his show in the dance troupe Harry's Hoofers.

'I remember when I first saw . . . er, what's her name? Never mind, it's the story that's important. Yes, I remember I turned to my co-star Benny Elton and said, "Tell you what, Benny, I wouldn't climb over her to get to you!" Ha ha ha ha ha ha ha ha ha!'

Despite being something of a national institution, Harry still takes a keen interest in the local community and has even established a sixth-form college for girls, where he is a regular visitor.

And his benevolence does not stop there. He works tirelessly for several well-known charities.

'I'd rather not talk about that sort of thing,' he explained to me. 'I don't want to appear boastful. What a man does with his money is his own affair.'

This modesty is further explained in the many adverts he regularly places in the national press thanking himself on behalf of the charities involved.

All in all, Harry Enfield is that rare find, a happy man. But did he have any regrets? I wondered.

'Well, I would have liked to play Sun City before the ANC burnt it down, but that's about it, really.'

So perhaps Harry Enfield really is 'the man who has everything', though he cheerfully admits to not knowing just exactly how much he has got.

'Honestly,' he protests, 'I don't know if it's £5.8 or £5.9 billion.'

But then, as I got up to leave, he turned to me with a tear in his eye. 'There is one thing,' he said Monkhousely. 'I'd just like to be able to go back to that dear old kebab shop in Hackney and order a large doner with extra chili sauce . . .'

LAUGHTER EIGHT WITH HARRY STARTS ON SATURDAY AT 8.00 pm. AND ON THURSDAY HE IS A GUEST ON QUESTION TIME WITH SIR PHILIP SCHOFIELD.

Dear Mr Beattie

I have just received-up my phone bill for the last quarter. According to you, it comes to £9,754.76! Are you taking the piss or what? I am returning it to you now for correction because some minion at your end has made one God Almighty balls-up. There is absolutely no way I am paying a bill this small, on behalf of I'd be laughed out of the pub. You must have missed something out. I mean, what about that 'Sexy Birdline' - you know, with Samantha and Linda and that. They've been ringing me up non-stop and reversing the charges. There must be few bob in that surely? And have you put in all me overseas calls? I distinctly remember one evening randomly dialling up whole strings of numbers and shouting, 'I've got an enormous phone bill!' to whatever foreigners answered. And I had a four-hour argument about football with some bloke in Hawaii, probly.

　　　　So, I'm sorry, sunbeam, but this pathetic excuse for a bill is like one of your phone boxes - yeah, totally out of order. I am a share holder, you know: I've got me rights. I wuold therefore appreciate it if you could at least double it up.

　　　　Yours

　　　　Loadsamoney

　　　　Loadsamoney

PS About the phone boxes, I've only heard that about them not working - I never use them meself, as it goes.

Dear Mr Loadsamoney

Thank you for your letter. Unfortunately there is nothing we can do to make your bill any larger. In fact, we have checked your accounts thoroughly and have found that we slightly overcharged you and are compelled to take £3.63 off your bill. You must appreciate that while we do everything possible to keep our bills inordinately high, there are certain laws that prevent even us from charging the outrageous amount we would like. So it is with great regret that I am enclosing your amended bill for £9,751.40.

　　　Yours

　　　R Beattie

　　　Mr Beattie
　　　Managing Director, BT

Dear Mr Beattie

You bastard. You scum-sucking, sheep-shagging bastard. You're filth, you are, the lowest of the bleeding low! I'm getting my solicitors on to you, I am, and they are EXPENSIVE. They're going to take you to the bloody cleaners, my son.

　　　And anyway I've upped my price. I want that bill quadrupled! Or it's British justice, here we come!

　　　Yours sincerely

　　　Loadsamoney

　　　Loadsamoney

Dear Mr. Loadsamoney

Thank you for your letter, you shit-bag. Don't you take that tone with me, you fat git. I hate you, and you smell. Your mother's a gorilla and your father wears dresses. You are a bloody sod, and you haven't got a willie. And just for that, I'm halving-up your bill, so there!

　　　Yours sincerely

　　　R Beattie

　　　Mr Beattie

Dear Mr Beattie

Right, that does it!

　　　Yours sincerely

　　　Loadsamoney

　　　Loadsamoney

Dear Me

Thank you for my letter. What a brilliantly written letter it was too. Now about this crap bill: since I became chairman of BT by buying up all the shares, I have fully empowered meself to up it up. How does £22,987,686.32p grab you, er, me? yeah, sounds great. I'll get my secretary Mr Beattie to type it up once he's finished cleaning Lady's piles.

　　　Yours sincerely

　　　Loadsamoney

　　　Loadsamoney
　　　New MD Loadsamoney (BT) Inc

PS Your letter was brilliant

WHAT IS LANCE?

Lance has been working for me ever since I discovered him at the bottom of a skip just off of the Old Kent Road. I soon realized that here was the ideal workmate, a totally clueless arsehole that I could ruthlessly exploit-up.

But just what exactly is he? Good question, and it's one that people all round the world are asking-up. Well, in a word, Lance is crap. I mean, he's harmless enough. It's just that he's a moron with the brain of a tree. Nobody could ever imagine just how utterly dense he is. But to give you some idea we are now going to take you on a journey into the strange and mysterious world that is Lance. The world of . . .

MINUSMIND

LOADUS LOADSAMONEYSUN: Lance, you have two minutes, starting now.
LANCE: Eh?

LOADUS LOADSAMONEYSUN: I haven't asked a question yet.
LANCE: Oh.

LOADUS LOADSAMONEYSUN: What is your name, Lance?
LANCE: Eh?
LOADUS LOADSAMONEYSUN: No, when you don't know the answer you've got to say, 'Pass'.
LANCE: Eh?
LOADUS LOADSAMONEYSON: Oh, never mind. Second question: how old are you?
LANCE: Eh?
LOADUS LOADSAMONEYSUN: I wish I'd never started but I have, so I've got to finish. Where d'you live?
LANCE: Me sister.
LOADUS LOADSAMONEYSUN: Eh?
LANCE: Me sister's birthday.
LOADUS LOADSAMONEYSUN: Oh, Gawd. Where d'you bleeding live, you daft git?
LANCE: Oh. Right.

LOADUS LOADSAMONEYSUN: Well? Go on, then.
LANCE: At home.
LOADUS LOADSAMONEYSUN: Brilliant. Now we're getting somewhere. So let's try your name again.
LANCE: Name? You know that.
LOADUS LOADSAMONEYSUN: Yeah, but do you?
LANCE: Eh?
LOADUS LOADSAMONEYSUN: Oh, piss off.
LANCE: Lend us a fifty pee.

LOADUS LOADSAMONEYSUN: No. BEEP BEEP
LOADUS LOADSAMONEYSUN: Oh, and your time's up. So, Lance, our freelance plasterer's labourer from 'at home', on your specialist subject of 'Lance', you have scored absolutely sod-all. Congratulations.
LANCE: Eh?
LOADUS LOADSAMONEYSUN: Shut your mouth.
LANCE: Napoleon.

The penguins, outside the opera house, after coming out the public house. Same difference really, singing and drinking and that.

Champagne all round. Always order up your half-time drinks well before the kick-off. And, remember, with opera you get a few half times.

'OFF-SIDE, PAVAROTTI!' But the linesman's flag stays down . . .

Half-time. Brahms and Liszt, waaargh!

More fighting.

Pitch invasion. It's all too much for the penguins.

Opening number.

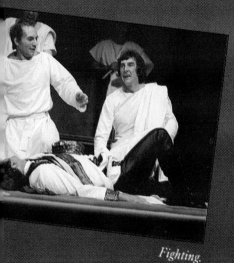
Fighting.

...lping the police with their inquiries after ...quarter-final victory over Puccinni's La ...hème, 'Total Opera' side.

A NIGHT UP THE OPERA

'Pavarotti, SHUT YOUR MOUTH!!!!'

That's right, opera. Opera is great, 'cos (a) it's expensive and that, and (b) it's great. Me and my crew don't go to the football no more 'cos it's too cheap. All that ever happens down the Spurs these days is I wave my wad at El Tel, he waves his wad at me and Chris Wad waves his waddle at both of us. Shut your mouth!

Yeah, we go down the opera now, our crew, all togged up in all the gear, you know, top hats and that, and we're called the penguins, 'cos we're brilliant. We support Domingo, right, 'cos he's the bollocks. So if you like Pavarotti, beware – you're dead meat for starters, mate.

OUR FAVOURITE OPERA SONGS

DOMINGO! DOMINGO!
DOMINGO! DOMINGO!
DOMINGO! DOMINGO-OH!
DOMINGO! DOMINGO!
DOMINGO! DOMING-OH!
DOMINGO!!!!!

WHO'S THAT WANKER
PAVAROTTI?

OH DEAR, WHAT A PALAVER!
GIVE US A KISS, KIRI TE
KANA-A-WA!

And so on. The list is endless, and this is the end of it.

One problem is that operas are all in foreign. And unless you know foreign, you're up shit creek. So here's a rough guide to the basic plot of all operas, probly.

1) General singing, crowds milling about, occasional violence, bird comes on.
2) More warbling, but only one person at a time.
3) Two blokes come on. One's got a high voice, one's got a low voice.
4) Mixture of snogging and violence. Half-time.
5) Second half. Crowd milling about a bit. One of the blokes has a bit of a sing by himself. Reads a letter from his mum.
6) Bloke with high voice and bird sing together, bit like Dollar.
7) Good singalong bit. Half-time.
8) Third half. Bird singing by herself.
9) Big bundle. One or other of the blokes, or the bird, or all three, die.
10) End.
11) Bird comes back to life.
12) Sings again, dies again, sings again, dies again.
13) Total audience mayhem.

Loads says,

'I'm not Jesus, probly.'

Jesus is, of course, that long-haired geezer out of the Bible who done a lot of good work for charity. He's chiefly remembered for being born in a stable with all animals and that on Christmas morning in the olden days. He is like me in many ways, i.e. Loadsapeople worship him, and love him and kneel down before him and that. But I wonder if you've noticed that there are a few subtle differences between us, which all in all add up to me being basically tastier than the son of God, probly.

The first thing you'll notice is that Jesus is only a drawing, but I'm a photograph. In fact, I don't reckon Jesus even had a camera. I've got one of them where the picture comes out the front. Here's some more differences . . .

HIGHLIGHTS

SKI JACKET

GOLD CROSS

BUNK AID

BONKED THE WORLD

HUMOROUS SLOGAN

ROLEX

WAD

CAR KEYS

SNO-WASH JEANS

NIKE TRAINERS

ME:	JESUS:
Born Bethnal Green	Born Bethnalhem
Mum's name, Joan Loads (Mrs)	Mum's name, Virgin Mary (The)
Turns lager into piss	Turns water into wine
Reads the *Sun*	Reads the Scriptures
Waves wad unto the poor	Ministers unto the poor
Watches man-eating zombie videos	Raises blokes from the dead
Feeds lambs to Lady	Kind to little lambs
Plasterer	Chippy
Loadsamoney!	Poor
English	Foreign
BUPA	Cures lepers

THE VIDEO EXPRESS

A service of Stav's Kebab Emporium and Video Club

So you've finally joined the ranks of all those other peeps who is a bit squiff after the pub and fancy a nice kebab and something to take your mind off it while you is munch. Yes, you is now a Video Express cardclubholdermemb'. And there is one word on that card that we is never forget. Tha's right, MEMBER (ooh, no, madam, please don' tit), and also VIDEO and EXPRESS – oh, yes, and CLUB. OK, so is four words that we is never forget.

We've got a wide seleksh' of vids, cater' to a wide variety of taste', from the adult to the innocent little kiddies, with such titles as *My Little Pony Gets its Head Put in the Liquidizer*.

Here's a few more of this month release for you to sit back in you armchairs and drink youself under the carpet to.

My beautiful kebab shop and video club
Dir: Her Inside the Doors
Starring: Stavros and the bloke from the DIY shop next door, who is pop in for a cup of tea during filmage
Share with the laughs and tears of a typical kebab shop own' in London's colourful East End as he sells four large doners and then hires out some of his excellent vids, such as *My Beautiful Kebab Shop and Video Club*. Shot entirely on locashe in Super-Eight. (With subtites.)
Video Express Rating: 10

Enter the One-armed Pole-vaulter up the Headless Ninj'
Dir: 新鮮な感覚で爽やかに描
No subtitles
Video Express Rating: 7 and a side ord' of numb' 23, please.

Enter the one-armed pole-vaulter up the headless Ninj'

Mad Axe-crazy Bast' Rampagin' Maniac in Pit of Hell Meets the Man from the Pru
Dir: Walt O'Disney
Starring: Dorque Plunger, Shane Savage, Brick Arson and Paul Eddington
Share with the blood and guts, and a rather slow end' involve' fill' out a lot of mortgage applicashe' forms.
Video Express Rating: 5½ per cent rising to 6 after three years.

Rocky 1 to Infinity
Dir: Sillyvest Stallion
Starring: as above
Share with the laughs and tears of the mumblin' moron Rocky Blubber as he's punch everybody peeps from here to Kingdom Kong. I'm got all the Rocky films. Well, actually I'm only got one – I'm just change the sticker with the numb' on it. Nobody is know the diff'. (With subtites.)
Video Express Rating: 1 to infinity.

Porky 1 to 5
Same as *Rocky*, only more violent.

Manon Depiss
The story of Buggerallmoney. (With French subtites.)

Ee, Manuel!
Sexy adventures of the lovable Spanish wait' from Barse, with John 'Don' mensh' the Germs' Cheese and Prunella Stales as Her Inside the Hotel.

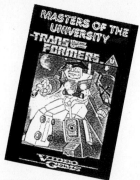

KIDDIES SPESH'. ANIMASHE' DOUBLE BILL
Masters of the University, Transformers
In *Masters of the University*, a bunch of quaint, bookish dons is sit around drink tea in the timeless tranquil surrounds of Ox' and Camb'. In the sequel, *Transformers*, one of the dons is transform' into a mad psychopeep and is go on the ramp' with his compasses and protractor. Unsuit' for childs.
When you is sick over you back teeth of this vid', you'll find you can transform it into an adequate door stop or tabe' stabilizer.
Video Express Rating: 3½ (could try harder).

Broadcast News
The news as broadcast by the BBC last night. (I meant to tape the film on the other side, but I'm set the vid' wrong.)

HOW TO GET ON WITH POSH PEOPLE

Areet, soah ye've pullt a posh lass, and ye've gaan back te hoor fancy howss, but ye find yesel' deein' fer a piss, like. Nah, if ye wanna creeairt a good impression wi' th' lass's pearents, it's impoartant no to piss y'trowsis. Soah, wop ye tackle owt, but divven jos' let it splash arl ower th'coarpit, nah. Sher a bit o' consideraertion, man! This is a posh howss! Ye gorra yoose one o' tha many recepticuls thertfully prervided in th' living-room aereah. As shern in the pitcher. Good look, and keep prattisin'.

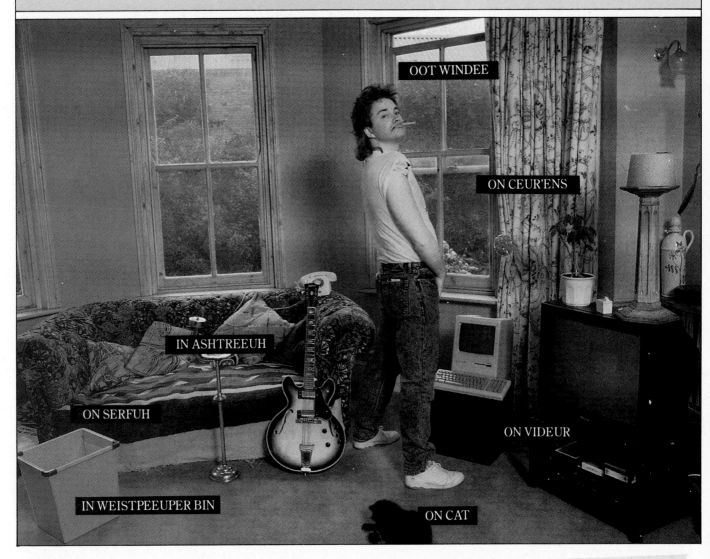

Hello, evwybody peeps, Hew–Inside–the–doows, Up the Awse, innit? And so on. Wewcome to 'This weally is the Last Wesowt, getting me in to fill up a page.'

Wight, my fiwst guest is a kebab. Hello, kebab. Is it intewesting being a kebab, or what, innit? Wight, kebab, thank you vewy much. That's all we've got time fow, as I've got to wush off and make anothew one of those cwappy lagew ads. Wewl, that cewtainly was mowe intewesting than anything on my last sewies. And, finally, can I just say, 'Wound the wagged wock the wagged wascal wan?' No, I can't.

Jonathan Stavwoss

Look I've had enough of this. I only agreed to do this page to get a plug in for my own book *Go to Bed with Jonathan Ross*. You didn't tell me you were just going to take the piss out of me in the most childish manner. I mean, all you're doing is replacing all the Rs with Ws: what's so clever about that? Jesus Chwist, I'm off home.

She loved the dark stranger

by Delia Diddle

ONE

She hadn't noticed him when she first came into the Grievous Bodily Arms because he had been hidden by a dense cloud of cigarette smoke, which had hung about his head like a curtain. But, as she sipped her grapefruit juice and slim-line tonic, her attention was suddenly drawn to him.

He was one of the most striking men she had ever seen. In fact, at this very moment he was striking someone at his table who had foolishly asked him the time.

She had never seen anyone quite like him. His jeans and bulging tee-shirt exuded masculinity and, even from the other side of the bar, a distinctive odour all of their own. There was defiance in the firm set of his mouth and a brooding intensity in his dark eyes, particularly the left one, which appeared to be closing over rapidly.

As if in a dream, she found herself drawn to him. And as she moved close to his table a change came across his features. A loud gust of wind cleared the pall of smoke and for a moment his eyes became bright, he straight-

ened in his seat and a look of eager intelligence illuminated his face. He seemed like a man who, if he so desired, could achieve anything.

She opened her mouth to speak, and in that instant his head slumped forward and hit the table with a loud splintering of glass and teeth.

An involuntary cry sprang to her lips. Was he perhaps the man of her waking dreams, suffering from some tragic and fatal disease, which he bore bravely and quietly, unknown to anyone?

Suddenly he looked up at her over the corner of the ash tray. A deep, throaty belch escaped his lips, and with one masculine sweep of his hand he wiped the cigarette stubs off his face. Before she knew it, he was on his feet.

She could see that he was wrestling with an inner torment.

'Trust me, my darling,' she said, almost to herself.

With one quick step he was at her side, and with several other, even quicker, steps he was past her and through the door marked 'Gents'.

Inside she was churning jelly. She sank down into the red imitation-plastic seat, which was still warm from his taught, almost lean hips.

Her head spun wildly. Was it possible to fall so desperately in love so swiftly? No man had ever moved her like this before.

Certainly no man had ever moved her before by bodily picking her up and hurling her off a stool with the words, 'Howay! Ah was sat there, pal!' As he did when he returned from the toilet.

TWO

The next few hours seemed to pass in a daze, but gradually the double vision cleared, and she became aware of his face staring intently down at her with a look of eager, questioning yearning.

'It's yower roond, pal,' he whispered.

Dusting herself off, she made her way to the bar across the bare, stained wooden floorboards, past the old, stained wooden club which a toothless old woman was playfully swinging around her head, and ordered the drinks from the large, stained barman.

She took the trayful of drinks back to the table and watched as he downed three pints in one marvellously co-ordinated action. Then, in a sudden, impetuous gesture, his arm was about her waist, pulling her towards him. Her pulse beat with a frantic, accelerated rhythm. Her lips parted and formed the opening letter of the word 'no'. But she was powerless to resist when she felt the strong, sure touch of his hand as it snaked across her thigh and into her handbag, from which it deftly lifted her cigarettes. Then, without removing his left hand from her waist or his right hand from his pint, he took out half a dozen cigarettes, lit them, and put them in the corner of her mouth.

She felt confused, out of her depth. No other man she knew could have done that. But then he was so different from all the men she had ever known. Neville, with his polo ponies and his hand-made Italian shoes, seemed only a dim memory.

And what about Peter Fincham-Jones, with his Giorgio Armani suits? Would he ever have explored her face so sensuously with his tongue in a vain yet gallant effort to find her mouth?

And then there was Giorgio himself, in his Peter Fincham-Jones suits. He had nothing like the bright, luminously radiant tattoo she had seen on the dark stranger's buttocks when he had mooned at her from across the crowded room.

And yet she knew nothing about him. Gently lifting up his head, she nibbled him behind his ear, dislodging several of the cigarettes he had put there for later. She whispered, 'I don't even know your name.'

His head turned slowly round to face her. 'Curry,' he replied huskily.

'I'm afraid I have to go now, Curry,' she said, hoping that her voice conveyed to him the right hint of encouragement and invitation.

'Reet, bugger off then,' he said.

'I was wondering if you'd like to walk me home.'

Perhaps he could guess from that apparently innocent question that her heart was consuming itself with a fierce but as yet unspoken desire.

'Oh, areet, get 'em off, then.' He stood up and began to remove his trousers.

'Not here,' she cried hastily, as he lifted her dress and propelled her towards the wall.

'Please,' she said hoarsely and gently pushed him away.

'Well, if yee divven fancy a tup, y'can take a hike, y'bastad.'

She knew that if she didn't act now, all would be lost, and before she knew what she was doing she smiled and petted him reassuringly on his curly perm.

'Why don't we go back to my place?'

THREE

They must have taken several hours over the slow, dreamy walk to her flat, even though the pub was only a hundred yards away. But they had stopped to have three or four fights and she had had to accompany him to the police station after turning over a police car while the officers inside were enjoying their fish suppers.

But finally they were home, and as she slipped the key into the lock, he pulled her towards him. She shivered with anticipation and pleasure – and because he had torn her coat in half at the back.

He pressed his lips against hers in a hot, burning kiss. It was too much: in the end she had to ask him to stop until he'd taken the cigarettes out of his mouth.

She opened the door and stepped into the hallway. His hands slid slowly down her waist, over her thighs and on down her legs until he was lying full-length on the floor, clutching her ankles.

Gently she tapped him with her foot. Springing up with a cry of 'Howay, the lads!' he swept her into his arms, carried her to the bedroom and laid her down roughly on the bed. So roughly that she bounced off it and on to the floor.

For the next few minutes, as she struggled to regain her breath, he searched for her on the bed until she clambered up to join him.

Then his lips were on her again, and she was overwhelmed by a combination of love, passion, excitement, saliva, beer, chewing-gum, tobacco, pickled onions, chicken fried rice, diced carrots and digestive juices.

'Bloooargh!' he whispered seductively, as his body pressed down heavily on top of her. She felt a satisfying warmth flooding over her as he quietly urinated down her leg. Then, in one deft movement, he unzipped her dress from top to bottom. She was momentarily taken aback, not least because her dress didn't have a zip.

'Why don't you turn out the light?' she said thickly, and in one smooth action he picked up the lamp, smashed it against the wall and jumped on top of her. She trembled as she felt the electricity flowing from him into her.

'Why don't you take your fingers out of the socket?' She murmured, between spasms.

'Divven mattah to me, pal. Ah'm *that* hard.'

Her hands moved down his chest, lingering over his proud, smooth, well-rounded stomach, then hesitantly, almost shyly, she stroked the firm contours of his hard, brown bottle, which he was clutching in his right hand.

'Take me,' she said.

And then it happened, and for the next few seconds they were united in a glorious journey into the land of passion. She had never known it could be like this.

Finally it was over. She gazed up at him and saw a picture of smooth, sensual nakedness.

'Please put that copy of *Men Only* down for a minute, won't you?' she murmured. He put the magazine aside and lit another packet of cigarettes.

He loved her, her Curry. She felt certain of that. Even though he hadn't said so in words, he'd told her in many other ways. The way he'd trusted her to look after his pint in the pub when he'd gone outside to be sick. The compliments like 'Ya divven sweat much forra fat lass.' And now the way he felt relaxed enough to fall asleep on top of her.

She lay awake till daybreak, when he got up to go to the toilet and she could at last move again. When he returned he just had time to whisper tenderly to her, 'Who the hell are yow?' before once again slipping off into oblivion.

She dozed off, snuggled up against his strong, pungent socks.

When she awoke, he was gone. She didn't know what time it was – he appeared to have taken her watch with him. But his presence still hung over the flat. His underpants, for instance, still dangled from the curtain rail where he had thrown them. Yes, she'd still have those to remember him by, she thought, and drifted back to sleep.

CHINA

THE
FACTS
ABOUT
THAT
VAST
AND
MYSTERIOUS
COUNTRY,
AS
TOLD
BY
ROADSAMONEY

Researched by H R H The Duke of Edinburgh

THE GREAT WALL OF CHINA

The Great Wall of China is the only man-made object that you can see from the Moon . . . Yeah, and you can see it's bloody wonky an' all! There's all them Martians and that, standing on the Moon looking at the Earth with their three eyes and going, 'Look, pleep, pleep, there's the Great Wall of China, kzark, crap, unnit? Blzzz, they should get someone to fix it up for lots of money, zoing! Like that totally brilliant earthling Loadsamoney, pwarrp! Sorry, I've dropped one.'

PYJAMAS

The Chinese wear pyjamas during the daytime. This is because China is on the other side of the world to what we are, so their daytime is our nightime. So they have to wear their pyjamas during the day, and when they go to bed they have to put on their Pringles and Lacostes, probly. Nutters.

N B The Japanese daytime is our bathtime, so they all wear dressing-gowns an' that.

FOOD

The Chinese all eat sweet-and-sour pork twice, spare ribs and special fried rice★ and something that they can't pronounce, but it's number 47 anyway. Sometimes they order up popadoms because they forget where they are. They only go out to eat when the pubs are shut, and they always have ten pints of lager, order too much food and pass out on the table.

★Watch out for Chinese rice, though, 'cos if you think about it, all them geezers out there in the paddy field all day long, all that water an' that all round them, they ain't gonna walk to the side for a piss, are they? No. I, therefore, recommend Uncle Ben's American Rice.

CHINESE WRITING

Chinese writing is different to English writing, which is why nobody can read it. As a result, the Chinese can't understand any of their street signs, and they're always ending up in each other's houses by mistake. Not that they notice, 'cos they all look the bleeding same, don't they, probly?

Also, as well as this, the Chinese populace always read from back to front. Which is exactly like me. Sports pages first, working backwards up to page three.

CHINESE DYNASTY

If the Chinese made their own version of *Dynasty*, it would be crap, or 'clap' as they would say.

BICYCLES

All the Chinese ride bikes and don't have motors. The reasons for this are many and varifold. But basically it's because they're a bunch of wankers.

The Chinese have hardly ever seen a civilized Western face, even though Andrew Ridgeley played there a few years ago-go

THE Scum

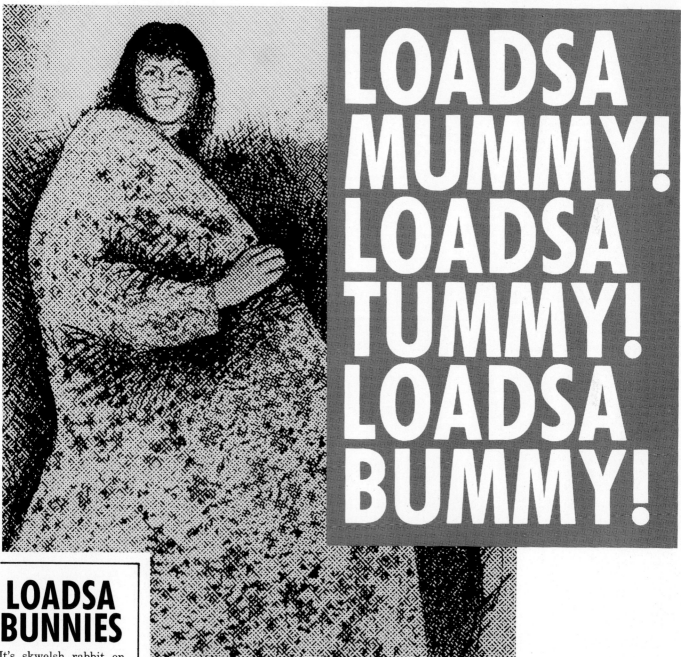

LOADSA MUMMY! LOADSA TUMMY! LOADSA BUMMY!

LOADSA BUNNIES

It's skwelsh rabbit on the roads of Britain, for it's estimated that over a hundred-thousand-million-trillion-zillion-quadrupled 'bright-eyed' bunnies are bashed on the roads of Britain every day.

Fergie has got a fat bum. And a fat tum, 'cos she's pregnant. God bless you, Fergie! We're right BEHIND you.

FULL STORY ON PAGES 4, 5, 6, 7, 8, 9, CENTRE PAGES, 10, 11, ETC.

INSIDE – Harry Enfield is a poof (probly).

"ONCE WE'VE FINISHED WITH THESE TWO, LET'S GET THAT BASTARD HERBERT SCRATCHIT."

BARMY BERNIE'S BENT BRENT BLACKBIRD BAN

Loony left-wing Brent Council have banned blackbirds from their borough. From now on they're to be known as 'birds of West Indian origin'. Anyone caught saying 'blackbird' could now be liable to a minimum trillion-year sentence at one of the Council's new lesbian and gay prisons. A leading Council spokesman said, 'We aim to finance this campaign by a staggering misuse of ratepayers' money'. Local resident Mr Alfie Codger, 93, said yesterday, 'It's ridiculous. My rates are now so high, I've turned into a lesbian and gay.'

LOADSAHONEY

FUDGEPACKER

Mrs Eileen Betts, 53, a packer at the fudge factory in Preston, Lancs, is a fudgepacker.

Britain's barmy army of busy bees are hard at it! There's nothing you can tell these stripy Romeos about the birds and the bees. In fact, honey production has reached epidemic proportions, and experts have predicted that if nothing is done to stop the saucy stingers, Britain will be engulfed by a tidal wave of sweet-smelling, sticky syrup by the year 1993, probly.

LOADSA BUNNY

Britain's busy bunnies have gone bonk-crazy! Experts say that they've increased in numbers by over 0.7 per cent this year. Which means that they've been at it hammer and tongs. A senior spokesman on rabbits, who doesn't exist, said, 'Yes, you could say they've been doing it like rabbits.'

LOADSAFUNNY!

"Blimey, you've got big tits!"

LOADSA NUDDIE

PM Marvellous Maggie Thatcher is not only an ex-virgin living with a married man. It's a well-known secret in Downing Street circles that everyday she takes her BRA and KNICKERS off and has a bath, STARK RAVING BOLLOCK NAKED!!! Good on ya, Maggie. We're in there with you! Page three awaits you, ma'am.

36

HATS OFF TO LOADSAMONEY!
by WINSLOW HITLER, the man who tells it to you straight!

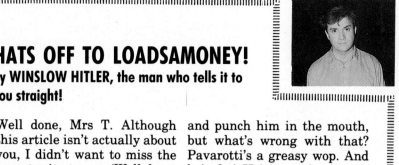

Well done, Mrs T. Although this article isn't actually about you, I didn't want to miss the opportunity to say, 'Well done, ma'am!' Today in Britain, all of us (well, all of us who matter anyway) have got Loadsalovelymoney. Hooray! You'd think that everyone would say that, wouldn't you? But no, there are still some people who don't want us to have our money. The so-called 'bleeding hearts'. Bleeding mad, I say! (Well done, Mrs Thatcher, by the way.) And where do we find these self-styled friends of the poor? Living in cardboard boxes under Waterloo Bridge? No, they've all got big country estates in the middle of the Cotswolds!!! These champagne socialists, Beaujolais bolsheviks, St Emilion Stalinists, I say they're all Filthy Phoneys!

What they can't stand is ordinary working-class people like you and me – could I have another of those truffles, by the way? – having money. The working-class lad made good. They hate him.

They say that Loadsamoney himself is an uncultured thug. My message to them is: Piss off before I smash your face in!!

Loadsamoney is the embodiment of all that's best in Britain today. He's a ma᾿ not afraid to stand on his own two feet – and to stand on anyone else's in order to do so. We should be applauding his initiative, not making feeble bleats about how wrong it is for the Americans to shoot down passenger airlines whenever they feel like it. (Not quite sure this follows on, but you can tidy it up later, Kelvin. I'm afraid I've got three lunches to go to.)

Uncultured? Don't they know that Loadsamoney regularly goes to the opera? OK, so when Pavarotti's singing, Loadsamoney has sometimes been known to get up on stage

and punch him in the mouth, but what's wrong with that? Pavarotti's a greasy wop. And he's fat! He's just the sort of greasy, fat wop who loves to come over here and eat our women and sleep with our food. (Another one for you, I think, Kelvin.) It was fat, greasy wops like him who invaded the Falklands, and it's people like Loadsamoney who today are carrying high that flag of the Falklands spirit. Hooray! (Well done, Mrs T.) My message to Pavarotti is: If you don't like being whacked in the gob, then get an English passport and go on a diet, you fat, woppy, fat, greasy, fat wop. (This is really good stuff now.)

We know who the sort of people are who whinge about our lovely Loads. They're all scroungers. They haven't done a decent day's work in their lives, and many of them are moonlighting with three or four jobs. (Think this might need a bit of attention, Kelv.)

But what about the people in the world who are much worse off than us? (Don't worry, Kelvin, I haven't gone mad.) The sight of the starving in Ethiopia was truly sickening. All those black people sitting around all day without making any attempt to look for work. Pathetic! Why should they be bailed out by us? Loadsamoney prides himself on not giving any money to charity, and I say, hats off to him. My message to the starving Ethiopians is: Get on your bike, commies! We're keeping our money. It's all ours. We worked for it, and we're keeping it. (That must be 500 words by now, isn't it, Kelv?)

Hooray for Loadsamoney . . . Falklands spirit . . . Initiative . . . Er, enterprise culture . . . Hooray . . . Oh, bugger this, I'm off for cocktails.

ARSE BANDIT
Commie comic Harry Enfield, who earns over £1 million every time he says, 'Loadsamoney,' doesn't just give no money to charity, ever. He's also a poof! Probly.

TONY BENNDER
His girlfriend, shapely, blonde Amader Name-Upp, 16½, told us, 'Every night I cry myself to sleep, but Harry just doesn't seem to care. He's too busy having sizzling sex sessions with at least a hundred hard-left Labour MPs, Arthur Scargill, Colonel Gadaffi and the Bishop of Durham.'

LOADSARUNNY
Britain's fudge is too runny! That's the message from European confectioners, who claim that Britains's fudge is not up to EEC standards. Leading British fudge expert Mrs Eileen Betts, 53, said, 'I'm a fudge packer, as was my father and his father before him. Now these moaning minnies in the EEC are claiming that our fudge is too runny. All I can say to them is "Fudge off."'

Buggerall's Barmy Bingo Bonanza!

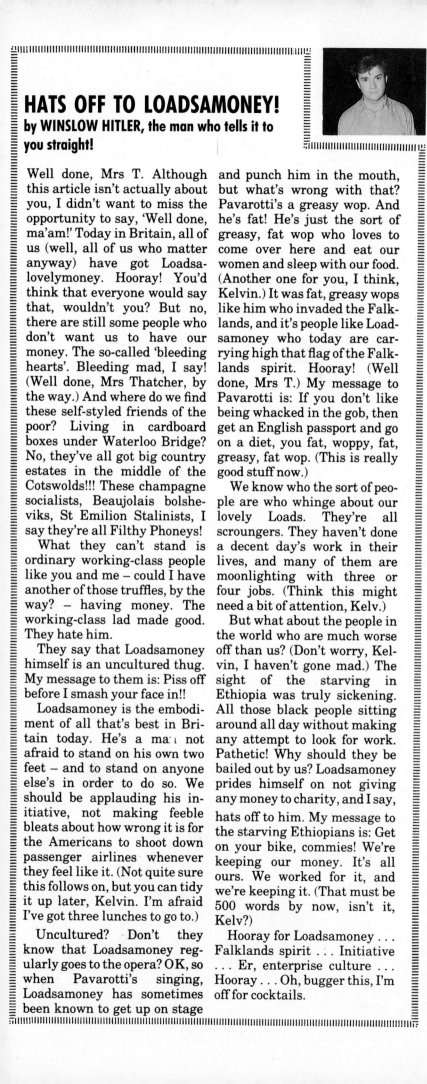

Raunchy paunchy Buggerallmoney, 27, says, 'That Bingoah's an owld woman's gayumm. Y'divven get naah bastad prizes from me, pal! Except a smack in the mowth. Nah piss off!'

LOADSAZXQONEY
Zxqoney, a new word invented especially for *Scum* readers, is due to hit Britain's streets tomorrow. Watch out for it in your local shopping centre.

37

HISTORY C.S.E.
LONDON EXAMINING BOARD
1977

NAME OF SCHOOL:
The Sherpa Tensing Comprehensive
(formerly the Sir Edmund Hillary Comprehensive)

TIME ALLOWED IN HOURS 1½
NAME: Loadsapocketmoney
DATE OF BIRTH: 30/5/61

PAPER ONE, GENERAL

Part A: BRITISH HISTORY
Answer all of the following questions

1. WHO LED THE NORMAN INVASION OF 1066?
Norman Wisdom, Norman off of Psycho and Barry Norman, probly.

2. DESCRIBE THE FOUNDATION OF THE CHURCH OF ENGLAND
Ground, hole, concrete pillar, bosh bosh, shoom, shoom, done.

3. WHO SIGNED THE MAGNA CARTA AT RUNNYMEDE?
Nobby Stiles??

4. DESCRIBE THE EVENTS WHICH LED TO THE COLLAPSE OF THE CAVALIERS IN THE ENGLISH CIVIL WAR
Alright, when they first came out the 1.8 injection was considered to be the bollocks, but then Ford came up with the Grandda 2.6 and what the bloody hell's this got to do with the English civil war anyway? That was all fighting an' that wunnit?

5. WHICH BRITISH INSTITUTION CAN BE FOUND ON THREADNEEDLE STREET, LONDON?
The Bank of England, sometimes called The Old Lady Of Threadneedle Street. The most famous bank in the world, probly. She is exactly 200 years old this year, so happy birthday ma'am. Amazingly, this greatest of all strongholds of wealth is the work of a man who began life as a bleeding pauper, Sir John Soane. Who was really John Swan, son of a labouring mason, of Whitchurch in Berkshire, where he was born in

Part B: WORLD HISTORY
Answer one of the following questions in not more than 300 words.

1. WHAT WAS THE EFFECT OF LUTHER'S DIET OF WORMS?
The shits, without a doubt.

2. WHAT, IN YOUR OPINION, WAS MOST REMARKABLE ABOUT MAHATMA GHANDI?
Even when he was old he still wore nappies.

3. GLADSTONE'S IRISH POLICY WAS DESCRIBED AS TOO LITTLE, TOO LATE, EXPLAIN
No

4. WHAT WERE THE PRINCIPLE GRIEVANCES THAT LED TO THE ITALIAN RISORGIMENTO?
Arse (I'm just mucking about now.)

5. DISCUSS THE ADVANTAGES AND DISADVANTAGES BROUGHT ABOUT BY THE INDUSTRIAL REVOLUTION, AND THE CHANGES IT CREATED IN BRITISH SOCIETY
Come on, let's face it, all you need to know about history is, they all wore funny hats and we won.

→ 1753. He was only 35 when appointed architect to the Bank of England. He rebuilt the structure, and spread the fortress for money over nearly three acres of land. The building has faults in the eyes of various experts but has countless admirers nevertheless. Right, next question.

Part C THE ANCIENT WORLD
Choose only one of the following options.

1. 'ATHENS WAS THE BIRTH-PLACE OF DEMOCRACY,' DISCUSS IN NOT MORE THAN 200 WORDS

Will I, bollocks!

2. DESCRIBE, IN NOT MORE THAN 200 WORDS, THE METHODS USED BY THE ANCIENT EGYPTIANS TO IRRIGATE THEIR FIELDS

See above.

3. DRAW A PLAN OF A TYPICAL ROMAN VILLA

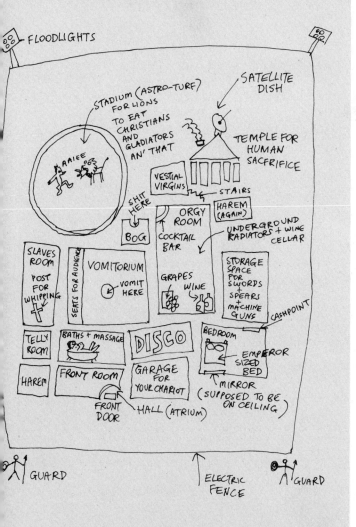

FLOODLIGHTS

STADIUM (ASTRO-TURF) FOR LIONS TO EAT CHRISTIANS AND GLADIATORS AN' THAT

AAIEE

SATELLITE DISH

TEMPLE FOR HUMAN SACRIFICE

VESTIAL VIRGINS

STAIRS

SHIT HERE

BOG

ORGY ROOM

HAREM (AGAIN)

COCKTAIL BAR

UNDERGROUND RADIATORS + WINE CELLAR

GRAPES

WINE

STORAGE SPACE FOR SWORDS + SPEARS MACHINE GUNS

CASHPOINT

SLAVES ROOM

POST FOR WHIPPING

SEATS FOR AUDIENCE

VOMITORIUM

VOMIT HERE

TELLY ROOM

BATHS + MASSAGE

DISCO

BEDROOM

EMPEROR SIZED BED

HAREM

FRONT ROOM

GARAGE FOR YOUR CHARIOT

MIRROR (SUPPOSED TO BE ON CEILING)

FRONT DOOR

HALL (ATRIUM)

GUARD

ELECTRIC FENCE

GUARD

DOMESTIC SCIENCE C.S.E.
LONDON EXAMINING BOARD
1977

NAME OF SCHOOL:

THE Sir EDMUND HEADCASE SCHOOL FOR NUTTERS

NAME: bUGGerAllpockeTMONEY
DATE OF BIRTH: 30/5/61
YEAR: 1977

Part one: GENERAL COOKERY
Answer all of the following:

1. AT WHAT TEMPERATURE SHOULD BREAD BE BAKED?
Oh bollocks, THIS ISN'T METALWORK, I'VE GAN IN THE WRONG bloody ROOM, me.

2. FOR HOW LONG SHOULD YOU COOK A FOUR POUND CHICKEN?
er... STUFFIN' AN' THAT. UP IT'S JACKSY!

3. HOW WOULD YOU MAKE MASHED SWEDE? GAN ower TO SWEDEN FIND A BLERK AN' PUNCH 'IM A LOT. THIS IS EASIER THAN METALWORK!

4. HOW WOULD YOU PREPARE A SOUFFLE?
Are you CALLING ME A PUFF!!

5. WHAT WOULD YOU USE A COLANDER FOR? TELLING THE F---- 'DAYS OF THE WEEK Y'STUPID BASTAD!

Part two: ORGANISATION

DESCRIBE A SUITABLE THREE COURSE MEAL FOR FOUR PEOPLE, ONE OF WHOM IS A VEGETARIAN. YOU MAY NOT SPEND MORE THAN TEN POUNDS.

HADDAWAY AN' SHITE!

DON'T YOU SPEAK TO ME LIKE THAT. NOW DESCRIBE THE BLOODY MEAL.

AREET I BLOODY WILL! — STORTER - BEER MAIN COURSE - TABS PUDDING - BEER AN' TABS AFTERS - GO OUT FOR A CURRY
NOW PISS OFF!!

Part three: PRACTICAL

PREPARE A 'FOUR SEASONS' PIZZA FROM THE INGREDIENTS SUPPLIED.

CLASSIC COMICS PRESENT...

STRUGGLE FOR THE POLE!

BASED ON THE LETTERS
AND JOURNALS OF
CAPTAIN R. F. SCOTT

PART 23 – WHITE DEATH

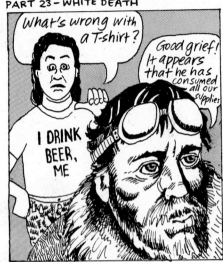

What's wrong with a T-shirt?

Good grief! It appears that he has consumed all our supplies

I DRINK BEER, ME

NUT!

Did you freeze my pint?

SEPTEMBER 12—WE FINALLY REACH BASE CAMP NUMBER 3...

At last, the chance of a restorative mug of hot tea.

Aye, and ah've ate all them wooly dogs an' all, I was THAT hungry

I DRINK BEER, M

But there was no friggin' beer. Lucky I brought along some of my own

Sir! I demand an explanation. We are the representatives of H.M. Government

Take a hike, y'bearded puff! I feel a punch coming on!

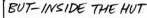

BUT—INSIDE THE HUT

Howay, y'soft bastads. What are ye doing wearin bloody anoraks?

I DRINK BEER, ME

SUDDENLY...

RAAARGH!

Shite! It's frozen solid!

Look out!

BEE ME

Ah've come at the North Perl, cos here everyone's a bloody southerner, so's ah can clobber the Torrayes

But this is the South Pole

I DRINK BEER,

Haddaway and shite! Everyone knows that the Antarctic's the North bloody Perl!

No—it's the South Pole and that makes us all Northerners

ID

The Antarctic's North, y'thick bastad!

South

North

South

REET! OUTSIDE!

BRAVE CAPTAIN OATES WENT OUT INTO THE SNOW— NEVER TO RETURN. BUT SOMETHING TOLD ME HE WAS NOT TO BE THE LAST...

I'm just going outside—I may be some time

Ah'll see to the rest of ye'se after

GREAT WADS IN HISTORY

Neville Chamberlain

Diego Maradona

Ben Kingsley

Winston Churchill

Mahatma Gandhi

Nigel Lawson

L**ds**

DERRIER

Why drink free tap water when you can spend a fortune on water that someone farted into?

NOW IN TWO NEW FLAVOURS – WITH A HINT OF CABBAGE OR A HINT OF EGG

CANNEL SEX

Hello, and let's face it, telly's a load of old bollocks these days, innit? So I've only turned round and brought a brand-new telly station on satellite, unnoi? Some people reckon that satellite telly and that is gonna lower standards. Shut your mouth! British telly's the most boring in the world, and, as Maggie says, It's up to private enterprise to put things right.

So here goes: the complete guide to your first day's viewing on Channel Sex.

7.00 **Good Morning Darling**
Presented by Loadsamoney, with a different lady guest each morning.

7.30 **Thundercraps**
Bathroom fun with Loadsamoney

8.00 **Vatman**
The caped crusader chases me around in a beaten-up Hillman Imp in a futile attempt to get me to fill in a VAT form.

9.00 **Play Truant**
I show the kids how to bunk off school. Plus a special guide on how to smoke fags for the under-twelves.

10.00 **Neighbours**
How to annoy your neighbours. I show you some of the most effective methods. This week, stereo speakers in the garden, parking in their driveway, noisy sex with the windows open, barking dogs and generally taunting them about how much more money you've got.

10.30 **Doctor Finlay's Cashbook**
Two Scottish doctors and their old housekeeper spend an enjoyable hour totting up their incomes, only to find it comes to a lot less than mine.

11.30 **Adverts**
A round-up of the dirtiest ads from around the world, including a few I've just made up. On tonight's show, Flake, Spa, Ambre Solaire and the Loadsamoney Breast Enlarger kit (that's one of mine, as it goes).

12.00 **Charlie's Angels' Charlies**
A chance to get a really good look at the bits of Charlie's Angels you really want to check out.

1.00pm **The Nudes at One**
A chance to get a really good look at the bits of Julia Somerville you really want to check out. Followed by the weather, with hot and sultry Tina Small.

1.30 **The No-Clothes Show**
Selina Scott hosts the popular fashion show in the way we'd all like to see her. Plus this week's special nude guest, the bird from the Flake ad.

2.00 **THE AFTERNOON FILM: Briefs Encountered**
Bored housewife decides to join the mile-long club with some serious nobbing on a train. Starring Felicity Kendall and Long John Holmes.

3.30 A Question of Cash
Bill Beaumont and Emlyn Hughes answer questions about my wad in silly voices. David Coleman sits in the chair, and I get to plug it in.

4.00 Highlights from the Eurovision Snog Contest
I get to snog lots of birds from all the countries of the EEC – and Israel who, although they ain't exactly in Europe I've allowed them on the show on behalf of they might have some tasty birds. Introduced by Sue Lawley, who I'll snog as well, probly.

5.00 Celebrity Mud Wrestling
This week Samantha Fox v. Linda Lusardi. And Maria Whittaker v. Mother Theresa.

5.30 Neighbours (repeat)
HELLO! IT'S ME AGAIN! WAAAARGH! SHUT YOUR MOUTH!

6.00 Nudes at Six, with Sue Lawley
Sue reads out the best bits from today's Sun, with nothing on.

6.30 Regional Nudes
Viewers' wives from all round the country.

6.50 What the Papers Say
A look at the current crop of Mayfair, Penthouse, Whitehouse and Playbirds with Sir Ralph Halpern.

7.00 Bob Says, 'Open That Trap Door!'
You pick which celebrity you hate most, and we kill them up for you, on live TV. And remember, corpse-makers, it's your vote that decides who goes for the long drop. On the show this week Gyles Brandreth, Francis Wilson, Wincey Willis, Su Pollard, the entire cast of Copy Cats, Richard Whitely off of Countdown and, of course, Bob himself.

7.30 Tomorrow's Wad
Scientists speculate about whether it's possible for science to devise a bigger wad than mine.

8.00 Three Up, Two Down
Starring Loadsamoney and his mates with several birds. This week's episode; Waaargh! Eh! Wallop! Err herr herr! by Dick Loads and Ian le Munnee.

8.30 Loads in Action
Same as above, only in an exoticer part of the world.

9.00 Film Buff of the Year
Compilation of lots of shots of naked birds from this year's more interesting films. A nice bit of family entertainment after all that politics.

9.30 C*A*S*H
Alan Alda and the rest of the team in the hilarious comedy about how much money I've got. This week they operate to remove an ingrowing tenner from my pocket.

10.00 Fwooarr! What's it worth?
The Fwooarr! What's it Worth? team investigate just how much birds are prepared to pay to go to bed with Loadsamoney.

10.20 Bath Time with Sir Robin Day
A panel of birds and Sir Robin talk about the news while they're having a bath, all naked and that (except Sir Robin), and then I get in with 'em, etc., etc.
This week's birds – Sue Lawley (she's providing the bubble bath), the bird In the Flake ad, her sister, any other of her female relatives, Tina Small (if there's room), etc., etc. Oh, yes, and Whitney Houston.

11.00 Nudesnight
Same as above but without Sir Robin and the bath.

11.50 Emergency Wad Ten
Hospital drama rather similar to C*A*S*H but with more naked birds in it, hopefully.

12.20 My Wad at Night
Patrick Moore peers at my wad through his telescope.

3.47 Patrick Moore finally
gets bored with peering at my wad and turns his attention to some other heavenly bodies. Including the bird In the Flake ad, dirty old sod.

3.50 Clothesdown
Selina, Sue, Tina, Felicity, TBITFA and loadsofothersaucycelebritybirds get 'em down at the end of a great day's viewing.

'Glasnost', 'Perestroika' and 'Smirnoff' are just three of the words I'm not gonna use for my political campaign. Why? Because I'm not a bloody Russkie, that's why, matey-voter.

THE GREEN PARTY (Bethnal Green)

The Bethnal Green Part' is the only real alternate' to the Tories and the other lot, yeah, the Conserves. Because, let's face the music, they is out of touch with the commonplace man. Oh, yeah, an' woman (Her inside the doors is kindly remind me with a big skewer). The Tory Party Peeps of Parl' is say they is understand what the man in the road wants, but I'm say to this, BALLOTS!

WORLD DOMINATION

Unlike Mr-Fats-Cats-live-in-Henley-drive-in-on-day-of-elecsh'-shake-all-the-hands-vote-for-me-so-nice-to-be-here-where-am-I?', I'm live local.

And, first and forepost, I'm stand on big local ish' like dog's mess. In fact, I'm keep stand in this partic' local ish' and is make me right hoppity-flip mad.

MY CAMPAIGN

Over the coming weeks I'm gonna be out and roundabout shaking the babies' hands and kissing all the mums (friendly snog on the cheek, no tongues, honest). I'm gonna knock on your door, rap on your window pane and have candy-and-frank discuss'.

And look out for me drive around in a van with a meg' shouting, 'Blrrwarvvnmmmmursssnwarr mzzzzn this Thursday!'

MY PRIMROSES

Sorry, my type finger is slip. Is suppose' to be:

MY PROMISES

I've been study very hard what all the members in the house is get up to, to make sure that I will be a model empee. So, if I get elect', I'm make a pig-iron guarantee that I will:
1) Bonk my sec'.
2) Spank the rent man.
3) Pay 2000 £££ to a complete stranger at a railway stashe'.
4) Make sure that Her Inside the Doors is very fragrant and is stand by me at all times (except when I'm have a Jimmy the Rid', of course).
5) Get very hot under the colander about something to do with helicops'. (I'm a bit vague about this one.)
6) Get on *Spittin' Im'* as a pupp'. (Pref a big one, not like little David 'I'm wet myself again' Steels.)
7) Resign on a point of prince', which I'm not quite remember the next morn'.
8) Find a book which everybody has read and then try to ban it.
9) Stand against myself in the next elecsh'.
10) Become so fat I'm have to have a whole front bench to myself.
11) Lie in the House. (Nobody is notice.)
12) Die in the House. (Nobody is notice.)
13) That's all my proms'.
14) Oh, yes, I'm nearly forget: blame dog's mess on last Labour Gov.

DUKAKIS X

As I'm say, I'm a local cheeky-monkey-sod-lad. And I'm been active in politic for nearly six month now, ever since my cuz in America is start to do so well. He's make me feel very proud, and I'm think to myself, blimey, that looks like a bit of a Ken Doddle, I could do that, innit?

Tha's why I'm ask you to cross my name, Stavros Dukakis, from you vote pape'.

OPEN ALL HOURS

If you want to know more, feel free to come down to our busy mod' headquarts, where you can have a choice of three size kebab, and try our new Jumbo Cola-style fizz drink. And of course meet me, your number one cand'.

Opening times: 12.00 to 3.00 and 6.30 to 1.00 (closed lunchtimes on Thursdays).

Let's work together to make the House of Commons the House of Commonsense. You know is make sense!

49

CASHPLOY
the new bored game from WADS AND TONS

Turbo-Nutter-Bastard
'Mine.' 'I want the motor.' 'I told you, it's mine.' 'You always have the motor.' 'That's because it's my game!'

RIGHT, THE RULES, OK?

THE PLAYING ACCESSORIES

Rule 1: The Bank. Personally I use Coutts, but you can use any bank you like. All the players should go to their respective banks and draw out as much money as possible. THE BANKER will be the person behind the counter who serves you.

Rule 2: All go round to someone's house.

Rule 3: As soon as you're having a good time, you know, beer and that, some wanker, hereinthereafter known as THE WANKER, will suggest a game of CASHPLOY.©

Rule 4: Some plonker, hereinthereafter known as THE PLONKER, will agree with him.

Rule 5: THE WANKER and THE PLONKER somehow persuade the other four, who'd rather be down the pub, that it would in actual fact be brilliant fun to play CASHPLOY.©

Rule 6: THE WANKER, who claims to know the rules, gives you a sketchy outline. And everyone else agrees that it looks like a piece of piss and 'Can we just get on with it?'

Rule 7: It is illegal to actually read any of the rules before the game commences, though THE PLONKER 'would prefer to.' It is important to tell him to sod off, or you'll be there all night.

Rule 8: All the players should be dealt ten pints of lager. The game should not start until at least five of these have been drunk. Then, starting with the player left of the dealer, they should all try and guess where the board is.

Rule 9: One of the players will now be designated 'unable to hold his beer.' And he will withdraw from the game in a hurry.

Rule 10: During the game, THE WANKER will constantly come up with new rules to suit himself.

Rule 11: Lance, heretoforeandthat known as THE LANCE, will always be in the bog when it comes to his turn. After a while the other players will get fed up waiting and take his goes for him. Six turns later, THE LANCE will have no money left and will be required to GO DOWN THE OFFIE.

Rule 12: THE BIRD, THE BIRD will start off the game quite well and will appear to be enjoying herself. About halfway through the game, though, after a few bad turns, she will announce, 'I'm not playing any more. Why are men always so competitive? It's only a bloody game. And it's silly anyway.'

Rule 13: All the players, including the ones who didn't want to play in the first place, will now say to THE BIRD, 'Oh, you can't stop now. We're in the middle of the bloody game.'

Rule 14: It will be decided that all THE BIRD's money will be given to THE LANCE, and he will be allowed back in the game.

Rule 15: Within five minutes THE LANCE will have lost all his money again and be required to GO DOWN THE OFFIE again.

Rule 16: After several hours it will become obvious that there's no way that the game can ever finish. THE PLONKER will say, 'Hang on, this can't be right.' And he will finally be allowed to consult the rules. He will then say, 'No, we've got it all wrong. I told you we should have read the rules. We'll have to start again.'

Rule 17: THE BANKER will now hit THE WANKER, THE WANKER will hit THE PLONKER, THE PLONKER will hit THE BANKER, and everyone will hit THE LANCE, because he forgot the cheese and onion crisps.

Money
This is not some ponce game with pretend money. We're talking real dosh.

Houses and Hotels
These are real and all.
i) Simple green house, with no doors or windows: 'Well, I'm sorry, love, but there was no doors or windows on your plan.'
ii) Stone-clad house: 'Everyone's having it done now. Only another £100,000.'
iii) Modern architect's house: The very latest in late twentieth-century design. Still no doors and windows, though.
iv) Lovely mock-Tudor mansion: Would lower the tone of Birmingham. Specially suitable for Windsor Great Park. Obtainable from Andy 'n'Fergie Inc.
v) Hotel: Five star, luxury suites, casino, loadsabars, strip show nightly, no doors or windows.

Designer Training Shoe
'I don't want to be the bleeding shoe again. I'm always the shoe. You feel a right arsehole moving a bloody shoe around, going broom-broom. I want to be the motor.'

Train
Customized-up. No seats, no windows, all graffitied-up. 'I ain't playing unless I can be the car.'

Ship
Comes in handy for shooting down Iranian Jumbo jets. 'All right, then, I'll have that.'

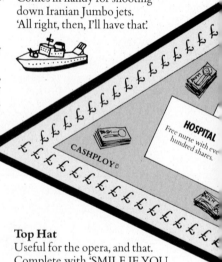

Top Hat
Useful for the opera, and that. Complete with 'SMILE IF YOU HAD IT LAST NIGHT!' sticker. 'Well, someone's got to be the bloody hat!'

Lady
Ha, ha, ha, haaaargh, she's pissed all over your hotel!

The Old button
Substitute for the other bit that always gets lost.
'Go on then, Lance, you can have the button.'

THE BOARD

Here's the board, or PYRAMIDIC PLAYING ZONE© as it is called. What you've got to do is, start at the bottom, pick a square each, privatise it up, flog the shares and you're ready to go. Then just move around the board, and that, any old way you want, like, privatising-up as you go and then off-loading-up your shares a.s.a.p. Except for some squares that are different, cos I got bored inventing it up, and er, well, you know, that's about it, so get ready for the off, come out fighting, do not pass go, (cos I didn't put one on), and when you get to the top of the pile you're the winner and you have to send all your dosh to me. (No cheques, please).

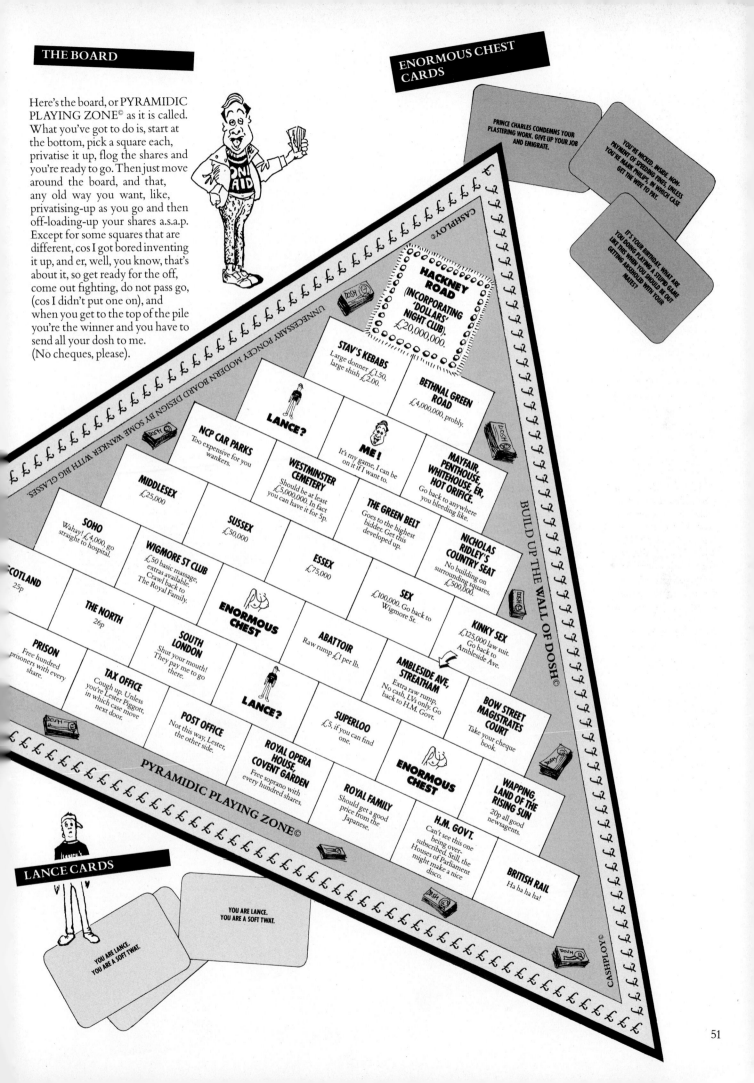

ENORMOUS CHEST CARDS

PRINCE CHARLES CONDEMNS YOUR PLASTERING WORK. GIVE UP YOUR JOB AND EMIGRATE.

YOU'RE WICKED, INSIDE, NON-PAYMENT OF SPEEDING FINES, UNLESS YOU'RE MARK PHILIPS, IN WHICH CASE GET THE WIFE TO PAY.

IT'S YOUR BIRTHDAY. WHAT ARE YOU DOING PLAYING A STUPID GAME LIKE THIS WHEN YOU SHOULD BE OUT GETTING ARSEHOLED WITH YOUR MATES?

The Board Squares

UNNECESSARY PONCEY MODERN BOARD DESIGN BY SOME WANKER WITH BIG GLASSES

BUILD UP THE WALL OF DOSH©

PYRAMIDIC PLAYING ZONE©

CASHPLOY©

HACKNEY ROAD (INCORPORATING 'DOLLARS' NIGHT CLUB). £20,000,000.

STAV'S KEBABS Large donner £1.50, large shish £2.00.

BETHNAL GREEN ROAD £4,000,000, probly.

NCP CAR PARKS Too expensive for you wankers.

LANCE?

ME! It's my game, I can be on it if I want to.

MAYFAIR, PENTHOUSE, ER, WHITEHOUSE, ER, HOT ORIFICE. Go back to anywhere you bleeding like.

MIDDLESEX £25,000

WESTMINSTER CEMETERY Should be at least £5,000,000. In fact you can have it for 5p.

THE GREEN BELT Goes to the highest bidder. Get this developed up.

NICHOLAS RIDLEY'S COUNTRY SEAT No building on surrounding squares. £500,000.

SOHO Wahay! £4,000, go straight to hospital.

SUSSEX £50,000

WIGMORE ST CLUB £50 basic massage, extras available. Crawl back to The Royal Family.

ESSEX £75,000

SEX £100,000. Go back to Wigmore St.

SCOTLAND 25p

THE NORTH 26p

ENORMOUS CHEST

ABATTOIR Raw rump £1 per lb.

KINKY SEX £125,000 law suit. Go back to Ambleside Ave.

PRISON Free hundred prisoners with every share.

SOUTH LONDON Shut your mouth! They pay me to go there.

AMBLESIDE AVE, STREATHAM Extra raw rump. No cash, LVs only. Go back to H.M. Govt.

BOW STREET MAGISTRATES COURT Take your cheque book.

TAX OFFICE Cough up. Unless you're Lester Piggott, in which case move next door.

LANCE?

POST OFFICE Not this way, Lester, the other side.

SUPERLOO £5, if you can find one.

ENORMOUS CHEST

WAPPING, LAND OF THE RISING SUN 20p all good newsagents.

ROYAL OPERA HOUSE, COVENT GARDEN Free soprano with every hundred shares.

ROYAL FAMILY Should get a good price from the Japanese.

H.M. GOVT. Can't see this one being over-subscribed. Still, the Houses of Parliament might make a nice disco.

BRITISH RAIL Ha ha ha ha!

LANCE CARDS

YOU ARE LANCE. YOU ARE A SOFT TWAT.

YOU ARE LANCE. YOU ARE A SOFT TWAT.

YOU ARE LANCE. YOU ARE A SOFT TWAT.

NIKOS MOTORS

nice peeps to do business wiv

Wha's the thing tha's get most peeps down in the dump-truck? Starvashe? The rise in fluctuate pound? The host' situashe' in the Leb'? The nucular arms race? No, is when you get out in the morn' when the birds they twit, you stick you key in the ignish' and you bloody monkey sod car won't start! Is a flipping noose or what, innit? Like the other day my old faith' Skoda one point nuffin' Total Notta Bast' is develop a bit of a rat' under the bonn'. I'm don' think is too serious, but I'm take it down to my cuz Nikos' garage for to give it one over, just in case. He is take one sideways long squint and say:

NIKOS:
Well, you know what the chief prob' with this car is, Stav'? Yeah, tha's right, is shit. Is a blood' Skode, innit? Boood' Brish Leyl' soddin' loadarub' mote no good on strike all the time hundred flippin' teas-break a day shoddy workpeepship rattly rattly flippin' bast' bits fall off go to sleep on shifts sod this buildin' cars for a lark too busy list' to flip' Steve Wright in the aft' and arf arfin' at Mr Mad ring up no time to build a quality mote' is another piss-bout tea-break, innit?
I tell you what I'll do, 'cos you my cuz, I'll do you a fave', I'm give you one hundred quids part exchange on a new mote'. Is a excellent condishe' Triumph Spit' one lady own' careful drive' ninety-seven miles only since new she's only use it for to pop down the shop for a pint of milk and then she's drop dead something about the exhaust pipe fumes get in the cock-pit, very sad. For her. But for Stav is very happy. Is a little beaut', or what?

STAVROS:
I'm thought Triumph Spit is a Brish Leyl'?

NIKOS:
Yeah, yeah, sure. Only no, 'cos Brish Leyl' is gone Japanese now, innit? You look at the new modern Roves and that, is all made by robes at Hond' from top to bott' very good qual' from the land of the rising currant bun. The only thing Brish Leyl' is done is pop the badge on, and that's fallen soddin' off, plonk, typical! Bloke who put it on is probly on drugs strike-me-pink tea-break asleep what this country needs is another war bring back Nash' Serve' and a taste of the cat, innit? Six thousand quids, on the nail.

STAVROS:
I don' know, six thousand quids is a lot for an old mote, Nick.

NIKOS:
No, on the cont' is very cheap. Is collector's ite' this one, everybody peeps is sell they Picassos and buy the Triumph Spits nowadays, no jokin'.

STAVROS:
Well . . . is a bit small for me, Her inside the Doors, the kiddie-winkles, supplies for the shops, salad, chilli sauce and everything.

NIKOS:
Yeah, but tha's where the easy-to-take-off roof is come in hand'. The old lady that's have it before is use' to run a bus serve'. With the roof open she's get hundred and fifty peeps innit, and still room for a little one on top.

STAVROS:
I'm thought she's only use it once to get milk.

NIKOS:
Yeah, well, everybody is want milk, so she's give them a lift, innit? Tell you what, I'm take off five sobs, 'cos you can't get the stickers off the window-screen, I can't say fairer than that.

STAVROS:
OK, I'm take the plunger. Yeah, I'm go for it.

NIKOS:
I'm promise you don' be sorry, Stav'. You like to use our easy payment scheme?

STAVROS:
Wha's that when is at home?

NIKOS:
You pay the whole lot at once, now, is easy.

STAVROS:
Well, I'm . . .

NIKOS:
Is a pleas' doing biz with you, Stav. Now then, can I interest you in another mote as well?

STAVROS:
No, I . . .

NIKOS:
Well, make the bugger off then. I'm got a livin' to make.

Buggerall's Computer Pintline

Just one of the many happy couples brought together by Buggerall's Dateline.

How does it work?

Forget computers. Buggerall's dateline is compiled using the human touch – well, Buggerall's touch. All you have to do is fill in the following questionnaire and within a week your ideal partner will be delivered, bound and gagged, to your own home.

It's as simple as Buggerallmoney.

D'yah have:
A) Good tayust?
B) A tayust fah Habitat fooerniture?
C) A distinct tayust o' beeyah and tabs?

D'yah:
A) Lake culture?
B) Think that culture's something t' dee wi' that herpless man-woman-man Boy George?
C) Have cultures groowin' arl ower y' feeyuss?

Are ye:
A) Cloarthes conscious?
B) Conscious?
C) Subconscious?

D'yah shag:
A) Witha lates on?
B) With difficulty?
C) Wi' just yersel' and a brerken bottle?

Are y' lookin' fah someone with:
A) Blonde hayah?
B) Hayah?
C) A head?

D'yah lake animals?
Howay, man, we're not intah that, yah dorty bastad.

Are ye fantastically rich, good lookin' and greeyut in bed, by the side o' the bed and on toppah the wardobe?
If soah, why are y' fillin' in this foarm, y' weeyudoah?

Are ye:
A) Fond o' drinkin'?
B) Fond o' drinkin' a lot?
C) Dronk?

Are ye:
A) A reeyall man?
B) A lass?
C) A dorty greeyut big goarls poarty dress or what, y' bastad?

Are ye:
A) Handsome?
B) Dronk?
C) Hoo d'yah think ye'ah, oarskin' arl these questions, pal?

Are ye lookin fah:
A) Companionship?
B) A ceeurin' relayershanship?
C) A Ponch in the gob? Ah thort ah'd tellt ye t' stop oarskin me arl these questions.

D'yah lake to drink in:
A) Pubs?
B) Public?
C) Brewah's vats?

Are ye yeesually:
A) Owtgoin'?
B) Thrern owt?
C) Owt fah th' count?

Are ye:
A) Someone who lakes the odd glass o' beeyah with meeyalls?
B) Someone who lakes the odd meeyall with glasses o' beeyah?
C) Soah dronk yaccoarn't read th' question?

Are ye the soart o' person who:
A) Is intah pubs?
B) Divven come owt o' pubs once ye've gann intah them?
C) Nevah leaves them in the foarst playuss?

```
NAME ........................................
ADDRESS ...................................
WEIGHT? BANTAM            ☐
WELTERWEIGHT             ☐
HEAVYWEIGHT              ☐
(Please tick appropriate box.)
I AM OVER THE LIMIT.
I ENCLOSE FOUR PINTS OF
BEER AND THE REMAINS OF
LAST NIGHT'S TANDOORI
CHICKEN MASALA.
SIGNATURE (if different from above)
```

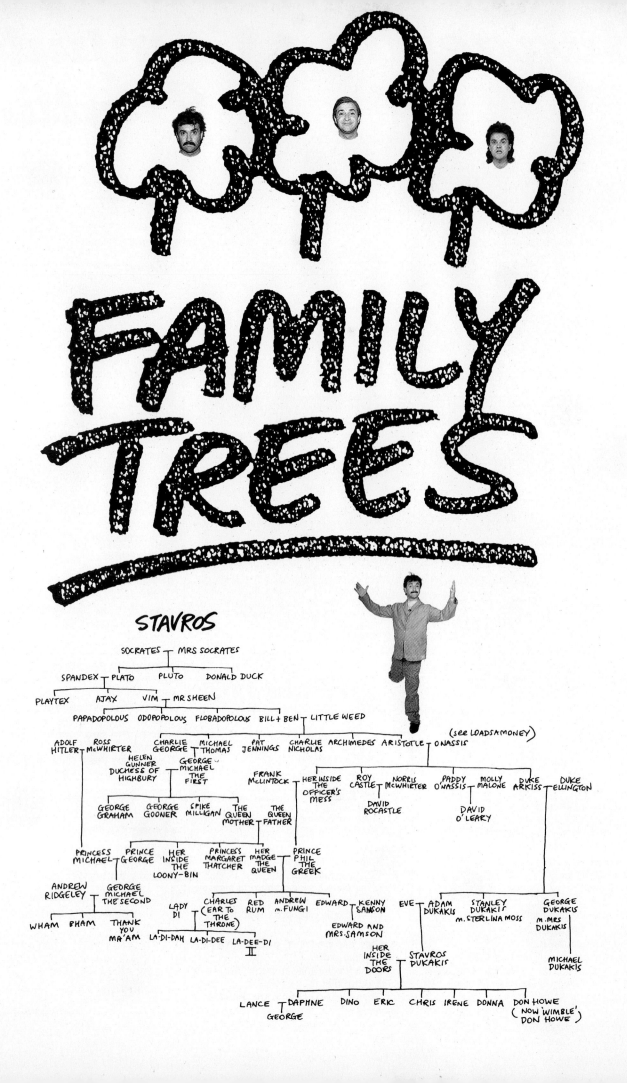

FAMILY TREES

STAVROS

SOCRATES — MRS SOCRATES

SPANDEX — PLATO   PLUTO   DONALD DUCK

PLAYTEX   AJAX   VIM — MR SHEEN

PAPADOPOLOUS   ODOPOPOLOUS   FLOBADOPOLOUS   BILL + BEN — LITTLE WEED

(see LOADSAMONEY)

ADOLF HITLER   ROSS McWHIRTER   CHARLIE GEORGE   MICHAEL THOMAS   PAT JENNINGS   CHARLIE NICHOLAS   ARCHIMEDES   ARISTOTLE — ONASSIS

HELEN GUNNER DUCHESS OF HIGHBURY   GEORGE MICHAEL THE FIRST   FRANK McCLINTOCK   HER INSIDE THE OFFICER'S MESS   ROY CASTLE   NORRIS McWHIRTER   PADDY O'NASSIS   MOLLY MALONE   DUKE ARKISS   DUKE ELLINGTON

DAVID ROCASTLE   DAVID O'LEARY

GEORGE GRAHAM   GEORGE GOONER   SPIKE MILLIGAN   THE QUEEN MOTHER   THE QUEEN FATHER

PRINCESS MICHAEL — PRINCE GEORGE   HER INSIDE THE LOONY-BIN   PRINCESS MARGARET THATCHER   HER MADGE THE QUEEN — PRINCE PHIL THE GREEK

ANDREW RIDGELEY   GEORGE MICHAEL THE SECOND   LADY DI   CHARLES (EAR TO THE THRONE)   RED RUM   ANDREW m.FUNGI   EDWARD — KENNY SAMSON   EVE — ADAM DUKAKIS   STANLEY DUKAKIS m. STERLINA MOSS   GEORGE DUKAKIS m. MRS DUKAKIS

WHAM   BHAM   THANK YOU MA'AM   LA-DI-DAH   LA-DI-DEE   LA-DEE-DI II   EDWARD AND MRS. SAMSON   HER INSIDE THE DOORS — STAVROS DUKAKIS   MICHAEL DUKAKIS

LANCE — DAPHNE   DINO   ERIC   CHRIS   IRENE   DONNA   DON HOWE (NOW 'WIMBLE' DON HOWE)

GEORGE

58

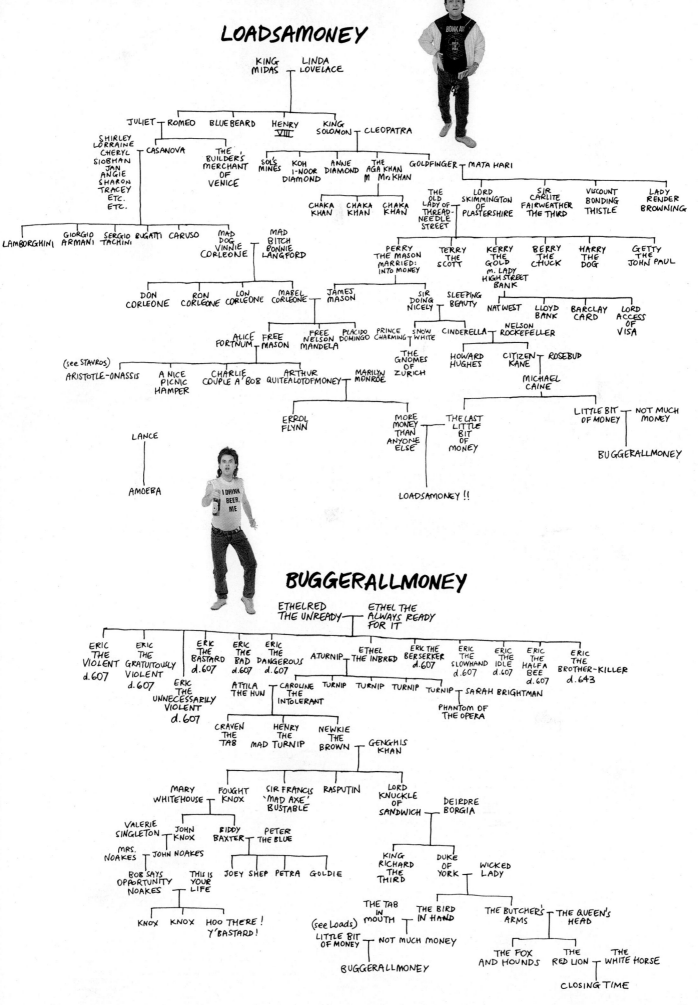

LOADSAMONEY

KING MIDAS — LINDA LOVELACE

JULIET — ROMEO BLUEBEARD HENRY VIII KING SOLOMON — CLEOPATRA

SHIRLEY LORRAINE CHERYL SIOBHAN JAN ANGIE SHARON TRACEY ETC. ETC. — CASANOVA

THE BUILDER'S MERCHANT OF VENICE

SOL'S MINES KOH I-NOOR DIAMOND ANNE DIAMOND THE AGA KHAN M Mrs KHAN GOLDFINGER — MATA HARI

CHAKA KHAN CHAKA KHAN CHAKA KHAN

THE OLD LADY OF THREADNEEDLE STREET LORD SKIMMINGTON OF PLASTERSHIRE SIR CARLITE FAIRWEATHER THE THIRD VISCOUNT BONDING THISTLE LADY RENDER BROWNING

LAMBORGHINI GIORGIO ARMANI SERGIO TACHINI BUGATTI CARUSO MAD DOG VINNIE CORLEONE — MAD BITCH BONNIE LANGFORD

PERRY THE MASON MARRIED: INTO MONEY TERRY THE SCOTT KERRY THE GOLD m. LADY HIGH STREET BANK BERRY THE CHUCK HARRY THE DOG GETTY THE JOHN PAUL

DON CORLEONE RON CORLEONE LON CORLEONE MABEL CORLEONE JAMES MASON SIR DOING NICELY SLEEPING BEAUTY NATWEST LLOYD BANK BARCLAY CARD LORD ACCESS OF VISA

ALICE FORTNUM — FREE MASON FREE NELSON MANDELA PLACIDO DOMINGO PRINCE CHARMING — SNOW WHITE CINDERELLA NELSON ROCKEFELLER

(see STAVROS) ARISTOTLE-ONASSIS A NICE PICNIC HAMPER CHARLIE COUPLE A' BOB — ARTHUR QUITEALOTOFMONEY MARILYN MONROE THE GNOMES OF ZURICH HOWARD HUGHES CITIZEN KANE — ROSEBUD

MICHAEL CAINE

ERROL FLYNN MORE MONEY THAN ANYONE ELSE — THE LAST LITTLE BIT OF MONEY LITTLE BIT OF MONEY — NOT MUCH MONEY

LANCE BUGGERALLMONEY

AMOEBA LOADSAMONEY !!

BUGGERALLMONEY

ETHELRED THE UNREADY — ETHEL THE ALWAYS READY FOR IT

ERIC THE VIOLENT d.607 ERIC THE GRATUITOUSLY VIOLENT d.607 ERK THE BASTARD d.607 ERIC THE BAD d.607 ERIC THE DANGEROUS d.607 A.TURNIP ETHEL THE INBRED ERK THE BERSERKER d.607 ERIC THE SLOWHAND d.607 ERIC THE IDLE d.607 ERIC THE HALF A BEE d.607 ERIC THE BROTHER-KILLER d.643

ERIC THE UNNECESSARILY VIOLENT d.607

ATTILA THE HUN CAROLINE THE INTOLERANT TURNIP TURNIP TURNIP TURNIP — SARAH BRIGHTMAN

PHANTOM OF THE OPERA

CRAVEN THE TAB HENRY THE MAD TURNIP NEWKIE THE BROWN — GENGHIS KHAN

MARY WHITEHOUSE — FOUGHT KNOX SIR FRANCIS 'MAD AXE' BUSTABLE RASPUTIN LORD KNUCKLE OF SANDWICH — DEIRDRE BORGIA

VALERIE SINGLETON — JOHN KNOX BIDDY BAXTER — PETER THE BLUE

MRS. NOAKES — JOHN NOAKES

BOB SAYS OPPORTUNITY NOAKES — THIS IS YOUR LIFE JOEY SHEP PETRA GOLDIE

KING RICHARD THE THIRD DUKE OF YORK WICKED LADY

KNOX KNOX HOO THERE ! Y'BASTARD ! (see Loads) LITTLE BIT OF MONEY THE TAB IN MOUTH — THE BIRD IN HAND THE BUTCHER'S ARMS — THE QUEEN'S HEAD

NOT MUCH MONEY

BUGGERALLMONEY THE FOX AND HOUNDS THE RED LION — THE WHITE HORSE

CLOSING TIME

Look, I done that page! Plastered it up myself – smooth as a baby's bum!

Marmaduke.

Have you seen page 60? Great page. Full of interesting ideas. Do you think there's a series in it for me?

Noel Edmonds

Can I just say that although I quite enjoyed page 64, it wasn't nearly as good as That Was The Week That Was. In fact, I don't think that anything else in the entire history of light entertainment has remotely challenged TW3. Thank you.

Ned Sherrin

WHAT A BLOODY RIP-OFF. I'M PUTTING MY SOLICITORS ON TO YOU. AND ANYWAY, PAGE 71 OF MY BRAND NEW BOK WAS FAR FUNNIER.

THE LATE M. PYTHON (MRS)

PS HAVE YOU HEARD THE ONE ABOUT THE DEAD PARROT?

Dear sirs and mad',

Is a stupid bast' wooden-brain idea to give a whole page to tha' lazy monkey-sod Lots-of-Money, the oaf with no loaf. Everybody peeps is know he's a good-for-nuff'. I'm bet he's charge you a blood' Fort Knox for do it, as well, innit? And anyway, I don't think he's very good for the chuck'. You can see peeps like that any night of the week down the rub-a-pub. Yobs with a few bobs, wha's funny about that? You should have give the page to that other bloke, you know the lovable comic foreign' with the funny voice. He's make me wet myself.

Yours sincerely,

Notstavros

Notstavros (honestly)

Hoo there, y'bastads! Let me onty that peeyuj. Ah wanna be sick, me. Ah heeyut poncy bloody designah white peeyujes. Do us a favour, mon, if ah'm no allowed ower there will ya dee some graffiti on it forruss? Heeyuh's a copple a'ahdeeyus for yee to copy owt.

ACAB

KILROY'S FUGGIN DEED
Cos AH BASTAD
Killed 'IM

BUGGERALL
TABS

BUM

West Ham
is A
PVFF

STAV'S POP PAGE!!!

Stavbros

Over the years many of the crop of top pops have popped in to my shop for a quick donner and some coke. I'm have the whole blinkin' bunch in here, innit, rock 'n' roll, soul 'n' rap and even roll and rat. All types is represent. That Melvyn Bragg, for inst', he's come in on his Red Wedge tour. Also some of the hard metals bands is come in for a bit of a Kerrang, like the Ironing Maids, Dead Leper and the Winifred's Girls Schools Choir.

Pers' I'm prefer the classics, tha's right, Tom the Jones, Shirley the Bass' and Slade. I'm think that Noddy is a great croon'. Mind you, I'm rememb' when he was jus' a little boy with a red hat and bell drivin' about in a little yellow Corvette, innit? But some of this modern poppy combos is okay.

Chubby Czecher

My fave' of the last few years is the one who is have Loadsahitalbums, as the saying she's go. But how comes I'm never see a pic' of them anywhere? Their name is NOW, you know them? I'm buy all their albs, they is all called the same name, 'Tha's what I call music'. So come on, *New Daily Express*, less have some pics, please, pronto.

The recipe for hit parade success this days is to go for the unusual combinations. (No, I'm not talk about the sexy boxer shorts, Paula. Take you hand away, you little minx.) You know, there was Busty Stringfellows and the Pet Shops, who is sing, 'I'm just don' know what to do with my shelves, blimey, I'm an old wrink', innit?' Then there was Michael Jacksy with Diana Ross, or was that Diana Ross with Diana Ross? And at Christmas we had Mel Smith and Griff Rhys Jones. Alas. We's even get Chubby the Czech with the Fat Boy, Elton John, and their big hit 'Goodbye, Vicarage Road'. Blimey, even Morris Smith is get in on the act when he's team up with Sandy 'Bernard' Shore. But I'm afraid I'm never forgive him for try' to put me out of biz with his song 'Meat is Murd'. I mean, what does he think he's doing to his fans? Cruelty to vegetables, or what? I should coke, and Pepsi, and Shirl'.

A lot of the kids is say that 'Hip-Op' is very trend' at the mome'. I'm a reck' Her Inside the Doors will be pleased. She's just have a hip op' herself, after five years on the wait' list.

The most pop' pop star today is probly my cous' George 'I want your specs' Mikes. Everybody peeps is think of him as a sexy love-pump, but I remember him when he was sit on his mother's knee havin' his nappy change all those years ago. Blimey, I'm even remember when Andrew Wrigley is have his nappy change – about two months ago.

But not a lot of peeps is know that most of George's songs was writ' when he was just a toddle'. I can remember him shoutin' at the top of his little voice, 'Wake me up before you ga ga goo goo, I want to do a poo poo!' We never thought it would go to number one, no, at the time is sound more like a number two. Phew! Pop 'n' roll.

Yes, Pop Picnics! There you have it, the wonderful worlds of pop. I'm gonna sign off now. As Her Inside 'The Doors' is say . . .

THIS IS THE END . . . DANG DANG DANG, BEAUTIFUL FRIEND, THE END!

Gary Glit'.

STAV QUIZ!!!!

Can you name the fame' Dave Bowie song in this picture?

(Ciggy played guitar.)

WITH

NELSON MANDELA

OF THE ANC

Nelson, you're one of the leading lights of the ANC and one of the most famous opponents of apartheid in the world. So can we start by asking you . . . if you were a domestic appliance, what would it be?
I'm sorry . . . I've no idea.

Never mind. You're obviously a very intelligent bloke, so, tell me, did you used to have any problems getting off with girls?
What do you mean?

You know, being brainy and that, did you find it a handicap getting off with girls?
I really can't remember.

Who do you think is better, Bruno Brookes or Simon Mayo?
I've never heard of either of them.

Well, I'd have thought they were both pretty well-known DJs.
I'm sorry, I don't know what a DJ is.

Blimey, you are out of touch. Don't you ever listen to Radio One?
No.

Hmmm . . . Well, that leaves me a bit stumped for anything to ask you.
Why don't you ask me about my time here in prison?

All right. Have you ever thought of forming a pop group while you've been in prison?
No. I've been preparing for the day when I am freed. So that I can help lead my people in their struggle. The struggle for the right to live as free men.

And in a way that's bigger, right? So what pics do you have on your walls?
I am not allowed pictures.

Well, where do you go at weekends?
Nowhere. I stay here, locked up in my cell. These questions really are getting a little trivial.

All right, then, let's be serious for a moment.
Good.

Don't you think it was a bit much not turning up for your own concert at Wembley?
I am not a musician.

Well, neither is Tony Hadley, but it didn't stop him.
You don't seem to understand that I am a political leader, imprisoned here for my beliefs and my attempts to get rid of the status quo.

Now you're talking. Some of us have been suggesting that Status Quo should retire for ages. Did you get a chance to see them when they played in Sun City last year, by the way?
No.

Don't you think all this politics is a bit boring? Come on, who's your fave hairdresser?
I've no idea who cuts my hair.

Well, it looks like a classic wedge cut to me. Now back to serious matters . . . You must have done pretty well out of your record.
What record?

Free.
Free?

By Nelson Mandela.
I believe you may be referring to the record _Free Nelson Mandela_ . . . and, no, I didn't make any money out of it.

Oh, come on. It was in the charts for weeks. You're not asking me to believe that you actually gave the record away free, are you?
I think I preferred it when you were asking me about hairdressers.

Well, these are serious questions.
I didn't make the record.

I see. So you're a bit like Frankie Goes to Hollywood.
Who?

You used session musicians just like Frankie Goes to Hollywood, did you?
Goodbye.

Now it's four years since that smash. When's the follow-up going to come out?
I keep telling you, I'm not some sort of pop star. Please – why don't you ask me about the ANC?

Oh, all right. When did you join the ANC?
1950.

And who was in the ANC with you at the time?
Walter Sisulu and Oliver Tambo. This is better.

And are they still in the ANC, or have they gone on to join other bands?
Look, I'm sorry: you are a very ignorant young woman, and I'm afraid I can't continue with this interview any longer.

What about an autograph?
Oh, all right.

OK, who would you like me to make it out to? OW!

64

PEDIGREE CAT

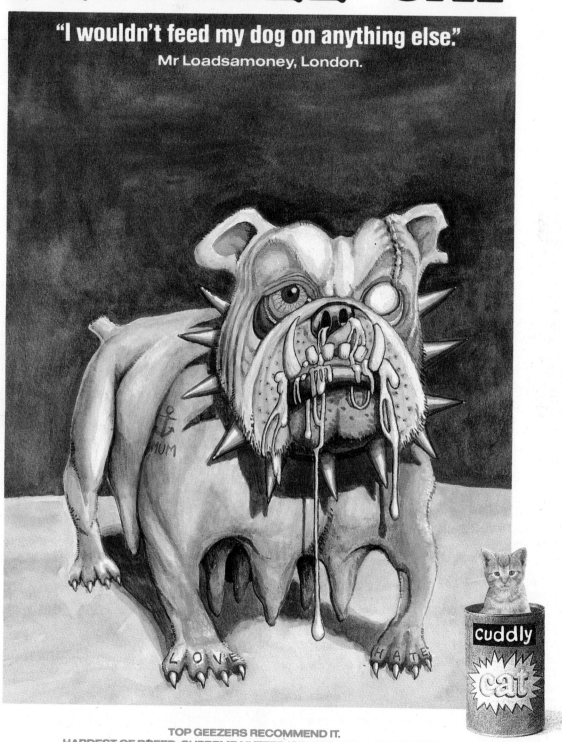

"I wouldn't feed my dog on anything else."
Mr Loadsamoney, London.

TOP GEEZERS RECOMMEND IT.
HARDEST OF BREED, SUPREME NUTTER, CRUFTS 1988, LADY C'MERE.
'NO OTHER DOG CAME NEAR IT.'

A DAY IN THE LIFE OF

by Alexander Soldyernissanyet

'BLAST.' Dmitri Alloverich swore as the loud wail of the camp's siren woke him. It seemed only minutes since he had finally got to bed after last night's routine prison-inmate count. In fact, it was thirty-seven seconds. They had cut the prisoners' sleep time yet again. Soon everyone would be working a complete twenty-four-hour day.

Everyone, that is, except for Ivan Enormouswad.

Oh, yes, in theory he should work just like all the other prisoners. But, unlike all the other prisoners, he had influence. And why did he have influence? Because he was the only prisoner in the camp who was rich. Not with money. No. There was no point in having a wad full of money stuck out here in the Gulag. No, Ivan was rich because he had pork fat.

How he wished he could have a wad of pork fat like Ivan's, Dmitri thought gloomily as he ran the razor roughly over his chin, chipping off the overnight growth of ice. Here in Camp Dismal pork fat meant influence, power and an extra forty-five seconds in bed in the morning.

Dmitri touched Ivan lightly on the shoulder. His eyes opened. 'Ivan . . . It's your early morning call.' Ivan nodded his thanks. Dmitri placed something by the side of his bunk. 'I've brought the shaving water.'

Reaching into his enormous pig-skin wad, Ivan took out a piece of pork fat about the size of an undernourished amoeba and pressed it into Dmitri's hand. Dmitri's eyes watered over. That would keep him going for the next few weeks. 'Thank you, Ivan Enormouswad.' He gulped (accidentally swallowing the bit of chicken gristle he had been keeping in between his back molars for later) and handed over the bowl of scummy water. Ivan sat up and knocked back half of it in one go.

It was another of his privileges. He was the only prisoner allowed to drink the shaving water with all its nourishing bristles.

Refreshed, Ivan pulled back his blanket, pausing for a moment to glance with satisfaction at the riot of colour. Grey. Everyone else had blankets of a colour so drab that there wasn't even a name for it. 'Paper come yet?' he called out to Dmitri.

'No, Ivan.'

Dmitri sighed. Another day of wiping his bottom on his undershirt. Like all the other inmates, he slept fully dressed, and having to strip down to his undershirt just to go to the toilet was a great annoyance. Still, it was too cold in any case. His bottom would probably stick to the seat, as it had done in the cold spell a few weeks ago, and it would cost him an arm and a leg of pork fat to get someone to chip him off. He'd leave it till later.

Easing himself out of bed, he buttoned up the single button on his overcoat. It was made from regulation material, horse-hair interwoven with potato peelings, but it had been personally tailored for him by Georgio the Armenian, who had been a top fashion designer in Moscow until he got twenty years for catching Brezhnev's little comrade in his trouser zip.

He carefully adjusted his hat so that the flaps came halfway over his ears in the fashionable way that he had heard they were being worn at this year's Volga Regatta. And, unlike the others who were forced to wear real fur, his hat was made of the very latest synthetic nylon fur substitute. Just another of the things that pork fat had obtained for him.

Pork fat. There was no doubt about it, pork fat oiled the wheels around here. And, as well as keeping the vehicles working, you could eat it, you could rub it over your face to keep out the blistering winds from the Urals and it came in particularly useful in the camp brothel.

But, for all his pork fat, Ivan still found himself every morning counting out the days until he was released. 'Surely, he thought, it can't be long now. There had been much talk of Gorbachev. Much of the talk was ill-informed and inaccurate. Some said he was the new manager of Dynamo Vimbldonskiev Akademicals who, by bringing in top goalscorers Glaz Nost and Perry Stryker, had dragged the team up from the bottom of the Lada-Skoda Conference to the top of the Soviet first division. Others said he was merely the General Secretary of the Communist Party, but from what they gathered he was engaged in radically reforming the country. Rumour had it that we were seeking friendship with the West and that we had even signed a SALT agreement with America. This Ivan could believe because salt had now become freely available in the camp. Some of the prisoners had started staining their foreheads with beetroot in imitation of Gorbachev, while the guards muttered that Russia was now adopting many of the ways of the 'decadent' West. And if that were true, then surely he, Ivan Enormouswad, must be scheduled for release. For, after all, that was exactly what he had been sent here for six years ago.

That was the time when the walls between East and West had first started to come down. Many of them had been built in a hurry under Stalin and, frankly, the standard of workmanship had been pretty shoddy. As a plasterer Ivan had been kept constantly busy patching them up, and with all the wealth he accumulated through bonus payments and what have you he had started to become quite a man of status.

People would start to whisper as he took his evening constitutional around Lenin's tomb. 'There goes Ivan Enormouswad,' and he would turn and shout back, 'Loadsaroubles!'

For a while he had been in the forefront of fashion. He was one of the first people, for instance, to get into anoraks with fur hoods. He had bought several of them on a trip to England, and his friends had been deeply impressed that he had been able to afford to shop at the legendary Millet's. He had been the sensation of the opening night of the Bolshoi Ballet's produc-

VAN ENORMOUSWAD

tion of *The Dance of the Omsk Hydraulic Dam Project*, when he had turned up in his Hush Puppies. He had a new car every two months. Admittedly, it was a Lada, and everyone who had one had to buy a new one after two months, but it still made him a man of substance. He recalled happy days driving round Red Square (not that he'd intended to drive round and round it for days, but the steering wasn't too good and the wheel had got stuck). He had been able to jump the queues outside the bread shops and go straight to the queues outside the wholesale bread warehouses.

But now he realized that by flashing his wad about he had made himself a marked man. He vividly remembered that day in Gorky Park when, tapping his fingers to the sound of his personal stereo, he had become aware of a set of fingers tapping that were not his own. And when he had tried to explain that, far from listening in on secret proceedings of the Praesidium, he was simply listening to the sound of the Police, they had whisked him off to the Lubianka in less time than Andropov's presidency lasted.

Although the charge of spying had eventually been dropped, he had none the less been charged with the equally serious crimes of Western decadence, undermining the Soviet state and possession of a Donny Osmond tape. One of the most telling pieces of evidence against him had been the discovery of his pocket calculator. The judge had been unable to comprehend why anyone should need a piece of miniaturized high technology to calculate how many pockets they had.

At first he had been sent to a holding prison in East Germany, where he made his position worse by protesting that he was as good a communist as the next man. The man in the next cell had been Rudolph Hess. And so he was transferred here. At first he had been treated the same as all the other prisoners, but gradually his experience as a plasterer had started to earn him respect. Somehow he could make the mortar go further than anyone else. Soon the camp officers started to call on his services for their own personal use. Such was the demand for patios and roof extensions that he could soon afford to be choosy, and to secure his services many found that they had to grease his palm with pork fat.

And because he had pork fat he had become a man of influence, and therefore other prisoners would give him more pork fat to use that influence on their behalf. It was a microcosm of capitalist society, he would reflect wryly to himself, as he warmed himself of an evening over a hot prisoner (who was more than happy to set fire to himself in return for a piece of pork fat). Gradually he had started to obtain a few luxuries, like snout. Admittedly, a pig's snout wasn't nearly as useful as a good lump of pork fat, but it was a start. In the mess hall he got a bowl for his slops. Everyone else just had them poured over their heads, and they had to catch as much of the slops as they could while they dripped down their faces. It was dangerous to go bald here because then the slops tended to just flow straight off and you were almost certain to die of malnutrition. And those weren't his only privileges: everyone else in the camp had to make do with just one pair of laces the whole time they were there, but he was especially fortunate. He had shoes as well. And he was the only one with a ping-pong ball.

But still, he reflected, as he spent the long day sitting in his deckchair directing the other prisoners who were working under him to instal the camp medical officer's crazy paving, time passed slowly here. The only recreation the prisoners had was Russian Roulette, and since no one was allowed a gun, they were forced to play with a home-made catapult and a frozen pea. It just wasn't the same.

The siren went. It was the end of another day. Easing himself out of the deckchair, he limped back towards the hut. The limp was caused by a great swelling of his left foot. Not that there was anything wrong with it. It was just that when he had first come here he had taken to sewing spare pieces of pork fat into his sock, and it had just become a habit. Now his left leg was three inches longer than his right one.

A weasely-looking man sidled towards him. 'Ivan Enormouswad, I was wondering if . . . you'd accept this slight offering?'

Ivan smiled as the man pressed something into his hand with a crackle of paper. The smile vanished. 'What's this?' he snapped. 'It's not money, is it?'

'No, no,' the man said hastily. 'Pork.'

'Pork, my arse,' Ivan responded angrily. 'Do you call this pork?'

'Well, pork scratchings, actually,' the man said nervously. 'I know it's a poor substitute, but there is a competition on the back, and you stand the chance of winning a Wet, Wet, Wet T-shirt.'

'What do I want with a wet T-shirt?' said Ivan, as he threw the packet away with disgust. He had definitely been in this camp too long.

Wearily he entered the hut and flopped down on his bunk. His hand slid down to his coat pocket, and his good humour returned. He had his wad. He felt the eyes of the other prisoners on him as he withdrew his hand. Slowly he lifted his arm above his head, and with a sudden, waving gesture he shouted, 'What's this?'

'Loadsaporkfat!' they replied as one.

'That's right. Loadsaporkfat.' He smiled and lay back.

That was the way he liked to end every day. Every day was always the same as this day. One more day in the life of Ivan Enormouswad.

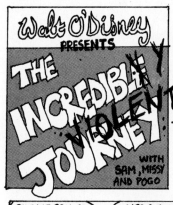

SQUASH

This gayum is *that* easy t'pleeyah. Y'gerra soothernah an' joomp on him until he's arl squashed intah th' peeyuvement.

FOOTBOARL

The ahdeah behind this one is to hit the boarll wiyah foot. Eithah boarll will dee, on any pleeyah. There's twenty-one uthah pleeyahs, an' if y'kick in arl foarty-two boarlls, y' win. Then y' can ponch the bastad ref, attack the herl crowd and gan doon th' pub.

DOARTS

Aye, this is a good'un. Y'drink twenty pints, smerk fowah hundred tabs and threr doarts at uthah people in th' pub.

SNOOKAH

This is very similah t' doarts in that y'have t'drink gallons o' beeyah and smerk thowsands o' tabs. But instead o' throoin' doarts at people, y'gorra clobbah them ower the skull wi' a dorty greeyut big stick.

SWIMMIN'

This is quite a complicayerted spoart, but good fun. Foarst, y' geeyutcrash a poarty. Second, y'see if there's someone smoarll that y' can stuff doon th' bog tah block it up. What with arl the people pissin' an' that, the bog'll soon owerfler and everyone'll be swimmin' in piss.

BOXIN'

Also knern as 'The Spoart o' Poofs'. To dee this, y' have tah be as weak as that gerl Mike Tyson, and y'have to weeyah daft shoarts lake a kid. And then yah arnly allowed t' ponch somepone's feeyus fah fifteen rownds, and yah gorra weeyah poof gloves.

REEYALL BOXIN'

This is pleeyud wi' bayah fists, brerken bottles and iron boars. Yowah allowed to ponch the other blerk in the feeyuss an' bollocks befowah remoovin' his back-bern an' snappin' it in front of the cheerin' crowd.

TENNIS

What's that?

RUNNIN'

The point o' runnin' is to catch someone and hit th' bastad. The werst runs are them big charity ones y' get on the telly wi' that Jimmy Saville an' Boowernie Clifton, arl dressed up as an ostrich, bastad.

THE ORIGINS OF MANKIND AND THAT

by Loadsamoney

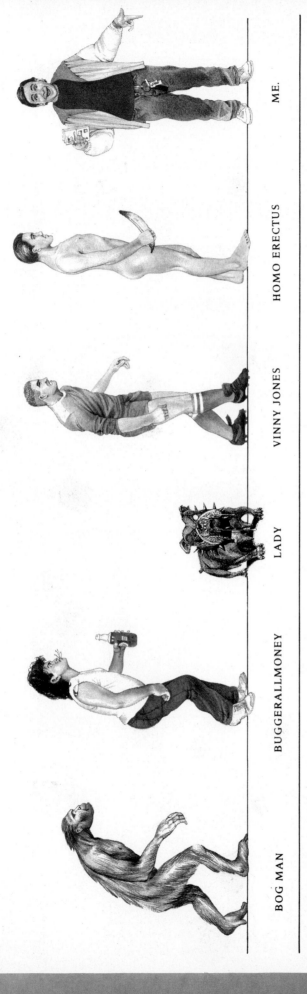

BOG MAN   BUGGERALLMONEY   LADY   VINNY JONES   HOMO ERECTUS   ME.

Right, this is how it all began and happened-up, like, so sit down and make yourself comfortable. Unless you're a bird, of course, in which case you can come round here and make me comfortable, WAAARRRGH!

Right, how it all started out was with bog man, probly.

Yeah, first there was bog man, and then there was me. With a few other bits in between, like Darwin and that, as explained-up above in my chart.

It's all there. Except for Chris Quinten – I seem to have missed him out. He wants to come in between Lady and Vinny Jones.

Right, bog man. He come out the prime evil bog. What was he doing in the bog all that time? I reckon he was one of them blokes who spend all day in there reading the paper and that, probly. Wanker. Although coming out of the olden days I doubt if he could read at all, as it goes. So, well, er . . . Oh, look, don't ask me, I wasn't there at the time was I? It was ages before I come along and was great, wan' it?

Anyway, probly what happened was that bog man come down out the trees, er, originally. In fact, what I should think happened is that he fell out of one of the trees, because he was pissed or something, and just, like, landed in the

bog, and that's how he become bog man. So then he come out the bog, right, he's turned round and he's got evoluted up. Eventually he evoluted up into man, and then right at the end of man was me.

But, right after bog man came bathroom man, I should think. I haven't put bathroom man on my chart on behalf of I only just thought of him, and I'm not going back to re-draw* the whole bloody thing just to put in bathroom man and Chris Quinten.

Anyway, that's the origin of mankind. And if bog man was alive today, there'd be loads of things that would amaze him. Namely the fact that all the dinosaurs

have gone, the England football team is still crap, the stupid licensing laws, and how much money I've got.

That's it. Shut your mouth!

*Actually I never done the drawing meself. I ain't got time to ponce about with pencils and that, have I? No. I got one of them designer arseholes to draw it up for me.

71

Daphne's Wedding

Wedding bells, alarm bells, you name it, they is all bloody chime out on the occashe of my Daphne's wed'. As you can see, I was prepared for to take some shots myself.

A hearty tradishe Greek recepshe for the ~~moron~~ groom, Lance.

The Groom's family.

The happy cup'. As they say, I'm not so much lose a daught as gain a grand-daught.

A lovely holy mat' join togeth kiss the bride fat and wide, except tha' Lance is kept say' 'Eh?', instead of 'I do,' until I'm whack him roun' the bonce with my trusty twelve bore. Look, even some of the men is so happy, Including the so-called best man, Loads, who as you can see, was very tired and emoshe'.

A particularly good likeness of Her-Inside-The-Doors, who unforch' was a little tippersey-turvey at the time.

The Nash' Health is very kindly lay on a limo, for to take Daphne and Lance on their honeymoon, at the maternity ward Bart's Hosp.

The best lager in the world, probly.

Daily Mirage

WED MAR. 2 1940

ONE PENNY

No. 14,093

FORWARD WITH THE PEOPLE

Registered at the GPO as a "No Nipple" Newspaper

A RIGHT PERISHIN' SKELLIWEG

Gotcha!

PLUCKY Czech freedom-fighter **Major Rzxt Mzxczvl** single-handedly repelled an entire German division at teatime on Friday, armed only with a rolled-up copy of this newspaper. Afterwards he entertained the British troops with Bingo. Brave Rob said to our on-the-spot reporter, 'I love Britain, and the British. Best nation in the world. When I've won this war, I hope to settle in England and take over.'

Wurgh!

That's my grandad that is, from the olden days, when everything was black and white, and that!

WHILE our gellent boys are orf fighting Hitler, others are staying at home, shirking their duty, and, through their nefarious bleck market ectivities, they're living orf the toil of honest folk.

This is one such chep, Charlie Couple A'Bob, from London's East End, where he cerries on his perfectly ceddish prectices.

'I'm a right royal rotten up-to-no-gooder, so fairly I is. The way I looks at it, that Mr 'Itler's doin' me a favour, droppin' his bombs all round 'ere. 'Cos, what I does is, I goes round and pays a visit to them folks what 'ave 'ad their 'ouses blown into fairly mortal disrepair and no mistake. "Why, look, Charlie" they says, me winders is all shettered, and I reckon as how me roof's a gonner, an' all. I doesn't know where me and the nippers is gonna sleep tonight, nor fairly I doesn't not."

'I says to them, "Why, don't worry. I'll repair you're 'ouse. But it'll cost ya, mind."

'"'Ow much?" they says.

'"Plentyaperishinpennies!" I replies. 'Then I goes ferritin' around the Ministry of "Ousin' depot, and I filches all the materials what I need, without not payin' nuthin' for 'em, nor never I don't. Then I just goes, shoom-shoom-shoom, bish-besh-bosh, 'till the 'ouse is done up in a right slepdesh Gerry-built fashion, so to speak. And they has to pay through the conk for my sloppy work. Strictly cesh. No benker's drafts, matey. Sometimes they 'as to cough up their 'ole life's savings, and if they doesn't pay on time, I duffs 'em up good and proper.

'Ah, I'm a right bad'un, me, and I got plentyaperishinpennies! Fairly, 'undreds of farthings. And I ain't not givin' none of 'em to the Ministry of War to melt down for bombs. No, I'm keepin' them for meself, see?

'Why, only the other day, I upped and bought meself a bloomin' wizard motor. Three-'orse-power Ford Prefect Perishin' Rotter. Twenty-five guineas she cost, and she does thirty-five mph down 'ill, fairly whizzes along, so she does.

'In the evenin's I gen'lly likes to share a joke with some pels in the public 'ouse while drinkin' too much ale. Then I goes out and cellously mugs decent folks and finishes orf me night beck at my place, fuddle-duddlin' with some floozies whose menfolk is orf fightin' 'Itler. Plentyapromiscuouspoppets! And I've got Plentyaperishinpennies!'

GU-STAV' HOLST'S
THE KEBAB SUITE

A MARVELLOUS NEW RECORDING OF
THIS PERENNIALLY POPULAR CLASSIC,
BY THE CYPRUS PHILHARMONIC
ORCHESTRA CONDUCTED BY
HERINSIDETHEDOORS 'FARES PLEASE'
VON KARAJAN, THE WORLD'S MOST
FAMOUS CONDUCTOR.

WITH:

JAMES GALWAY
WHISTLE AND FLUTE

LEON GOOSENS
STUFFED OBOEGINES

EDWARD HEATH
ORGAN

MINCED LAMB
UNIDENTIFIABLE ORGAN

CAPTAIN BIRD'S EYE
BASS

FRESH TODAY
GRILLED SEA BASS

FEATURING SUCH WELL-LOVED PIECES AS
'DONNER', 'SHISH', 'SHASHLIK', AND THE
EXCITING 'EXTRA CHILLI SAUCE, PLEASE'.

AVAILABLE IN THREE SIZES, ALBUM,
CASSETTE AND CD (ALL WITH SALAD).
ONLY FROM ARSE RECORDS.

OTHER TITLES IN THIS SERIES INCLUDE:
PROKOVIEV'S 'PITTA AND THE
WOLF,' **SIBELIUS'** 'KARELIA SWEET'
(WITH CREAM), **TITO GOBBI** SINGS
YOUR FAVOURITE ARIAS, INCLUDING
'LA DONNER È MOBILÈ', 'NESSUN DONNER'
AND 'STUFFED FIGAROS'
'LOHENBRAU' (DRAFT) **WAGNER**
'WINE' **LISZT**
(TAKE-AWAYS AVAILABLE.)

Things to shout at celebrities

Some useful tips from Loadsa-Egon-Monay for the rowdy diner. When you eat out in tasty restaurants as much as I do – and, let's face it, we're talking anything up to fifteen times a day and with fifteen different birds – you're bound to bump into a few minor celebrities ('cos no one's major compared up to me). And, take it from me, when they're having a quiet meal with their loved ones, there's nuffin' they like more better than having members of the public acknowledgin' their presence in a loud and boisterous manner. They love it!

There are two basic lines which you can use to shout at anyone who's a celebrity:
OI, IT'S YOU, ISN'T IT? IT IS, ISN'T IT? BLOODY HELL, IT IS YOU! OH, MY BLEEDING GOD! OI, LOOK WHO IT IS! BLOODY HELL!
And:
HOW COME YOU'RE MUCH BIGGER ON THE TELLY?
But it always helps to give the personal touch. Your average celebrity really appreciates a bit of wit in a greeting specially tailored to his or her own individual personality. Here's some good things to shout that have served me well over the years. Good luck and bon voyage!

PRINCE CHARLES:
AL RIGHT, FLAPPERS? ARE YOU TALKING TO THE SALAD AGAIN? HAR, HAR.

PRINCESS ANNE:
OI, YOU LOOK JUST LIKE PRINCESS ANNE!

BOY GEORGE:
OI, GEORGE, I BET YOU DON'T KNOW WHETHER TO USE THE GENTS OR THE LADIES, HA, HA.

RALPH HALPERN:
I'VE GOT MORE MONEY THAN YOU, MATE, AND BIRDS.

MARTINA NAVRATILOVA:
OI, NAVRATIWHATEVERYOURN-AMEIS? I RECKON THE ONLY REASON YOU'RE A LESBIAN IS 'COS YOU HAVEN'T MET ME YET, PROBLY.

ROWAN ATKINSON:
OI, BIG-NOSE, WHERE'S THE FUNNY ONE, THEN? YOU KNOW – BALDRICK. HAR, HAR, HAR. WHERE'S BALDRICK, THEN?

JAN LEEMING:
OI, JAN, LOVE, HERE YOU ARE – AUTOGRAPH ME BUM. GO ON. WAIT'LL I SHOW THIS TO THE BLOKES AT WORK.

RONNIE BARKER:
HOW MUCH YOU GIVE ME FOR THIS STEAK? ONLY I RECKON IT'S A BLEEDIN' ANTIQUE, MESELF. HA, HA.

JONATHAN ROSS:
YOUR NEW SEWIES IS CWAP, MATE. RANKER!

ALED JONES:
HEY, ALED, YOUR BALLS DROPPED YET THEN OR WHAT? YAAARGH!

MIKE TYSON:
COME AND HAVE A GO IF YOU THINK YOU'RE HARD ENOUGH. OUCH.

POPE JOHN PAUL:
WHERE'S GEORGE AND
RINGO, WOOORGH?

HARRY ENFIELD:
OI, MATE, I BET YOU GOT
LOADSAMONEY NOW, HA, HA.
HOW COME YOU'RE A LEFTY,
EH? WITH ALL THAT MONEY?
EH? LOADSAMONEYYYY!!!!

VALERIE SINGLETON:
GET 'EM OFF.

PAMELA STEPHENSON:
OH, BLIMEY, PUT EM BACK
ON, DARLING.

**FRANCIS WILSON (THE
WEATHER MAN):**
PISS OFF AND DIE, YOU
BASTARD.

STAVGAG

SOME OF THESE KIDDIES TOYS IS BLOODY DANGE' INNIT? LOOK AT THIS BABIES RUGGER-BEE BALL FROM TAIWAN, IS LOOK HARMLESS ENOUGH...

BUT THIS BIT IS PULL OUT AND THERE IS A VERY NASTY PIN ON IT; IS A FLIPPIN' SCAND!...A LITTLE CHILD COULD TAKE AN EYE OUT, INNIT!

BLAM!

DRIVE INTO THE FUTURE IN THE NEW
ROADS
convertible

Are you hard enough to drive the new **ROADSHAGGER MTNB?** The car for which the word 'MOTORWAY MAYHEM' was invented, not to mention CARNAGE. With its vertical take-off and landing, its revolutionary, extra loud 'Mad-Dog' Colander® exhaust system and its ear-splitting 'Rogue Elephant' Billion Decibel musical horn, you're sure to be the Talk of the Town, (and the subject of various legal actions under the Control of Pollution Act).

You haven't lived until you've driven the **ROADSHAGGER MTNB.** Just look at these EXTRAS which come as STANDARD:
● Heated rear window with wiper and choice of amusing stickers.
● 'Too pissed to remember where you've parked' homing device.
● Genuine freshly clubbed baby seal skin seatcovers.
● Three bogs! Upstairs bog, downstairs bog and disco bog.
● Cashpoint machine with automatic statement.
● Infra-red night-vision system for your heat-seeking missiles.
● King-sized waterbed with 'rear-view' mirror.
● TV with satellite dish (for all that Italian football).
● Video with range of 'interesting' tapes (including all those sexy Italian MPs).
● Mirrored ceiling.

The only thing we don't supply is the birds! That's up to you, sunbeam.

And the Roadshagger has a number of exclusive features that you'll find on no other car. Like the revolutionary new 'Cyclist Deterrent'. Yes, the Queen Boadicea™ revolving hub swords allow you to clear the road at the flick of a switch.

AND THAT'S NOT ALL! Every Roadshagger comes fully equipped with 100% tungsten, explosive-tipped bumpers. When you drive into people, they'll really know it!

Other cars may try and tempt you with quadrophonic sound. But with the Roadshagger's massive six-speaker 'YOU WHAT?' SEX-A-PHONIC SOUND SYSTEM, you'll really be able to hear Billy Ocean, and so will everybody else within a ten-mile radius. Yes, the only thing louder than the tape machine is the horn. Or should we say BRASS SECTION? Because you've got the Royal Philharmonic under the bonnet, with a full repertoire of classical tunes, Colonel Bogey, La Cucaracha, Dixie and many more. And, what's more, every ONE note in FOUR is WRONG.

But what about the engine? All you need to know is IT'S BIG AND IT'S LOUD, and it does about a hundred yards to the gallon, so you'll be able to spend plenty of time in the garage, showing off your wad and showing out to the ladies.

As you can imagine, an engine like the Roadshagger's needs an ostentatious gear system. And they don't come any more ostentatious than the **ROADSHAGGER'S** unique BIG SEVEN gear box. Yes, that's **seven** gears, fourth, fifth, sixth, reverse, up, submerge, hyper-space and eight. Yes, **eight.** Even while you've been reading this, we've added a new gear. In the Roadshagger you'll arrive at your destination before you've even left home.

And you're guaranteed screaming tyres every time YOU PULL AWAY with our MAD BABOON DYNAMIC INSTA-SQUEAL feature. (Optional wheelie facility on deluxe models.)

More power under the bonnet than a Mexican earthquake, and that's just the hooter!

AR5E

80

MEGA-TURBO-NUTTER-BASTARD
HAGGER

'I wouldn't run over pedestrians in any other motor.'
Mr Loadsamoney, London.

In the words of one motoring correspondent, the Roadshagger's engine is 'the Bollocks!' And our scientists are constantly working to add new features, such as the unique alcohol injection system that allows the Roadshagger to run on lager. And not just Regular Lager – Extra! TENNANT'S EXTRA!

Yes, driving's a pleasure again with the Roadshagger. We've even built in a computerized voice synthesizer which actually gives you driving tips as you race along.

Getting close to the driver in front? The on-board computer will tell you, 'Go on, cut the bastard up!'

Yes, it's programmed with the full range of driving hints, including 'Check out the bird in the Ferrari', 'Get a load of the arse on that', 'Hospital. Let's wake those National Health bastards up', and 'Die, learner.'

And if you go for the Roadshagger Mega-Turbo-Nutter-Bastard 'De luxe,'* you'll be able to enjoy it's self-cleaning radiator grille, which saves you the bother of removing all those tiresome insects, twigs, cats and dogs, Minis and police officers.

PLUS the fake safety belt. Simply rest it across your stomach. To the casual observer it looks just like the real thing, but it gives you NONE OF THE PROTECTION of an ordinary seat belt.

TEMPTED UP?
Then why not pop down to your local dealer and 'Test-Drive' a **ROADSHAGGER** today† – if you've got a big enough wad, that is.

*All Deluxe models are fitted with retro-rockets (batteries not included).
†Subject to Air Traffic Control clearance.

FLAME THROWER,   BOADICEA,   EJECTOR SEAT,
RADAR,   CIGARETTE LIGHTER,
SURFACE TO AIR
MISSILE LAUNCHER,

Drinks cabinet.

The Roadshagger's car-phone.

The Highwayman's Code
by LOADSAMONEY

An Englishman's motor is his castle, as the saying goes. But when it comes to driving, your average British motorist doesn't know his arse from his portcullis. So here's my guide to driving out and about.

Here goes.

GENERAL

1 Get yourself a decent set of wheels.

2 You might care to get yourself taxed-up and insured-up, but this is optional.

3 Before pulling away, check the mirror to make sure there's a couple of tasty birds in your motor.

4 Always drive at twenty miles an hour over the speed limit except, of course, when there is thick fog or torrential rain, in which case you should drive at thirty miles an hour over it.

5 When approaching a roundabout, accelerate and start looking for a cassette in your glove compartment.

6 In the highly unlikely event of being stopped at a traffic light, rev your engine up as loud as possible and throw litter an' that out the window.

7 If you come across a traffic snarl-up caused by another 'motorist', be sure to stick your head out and shout, 'I bet that's a bird!'

8 Always make sure that your car alarm's set to go off at five in the morning when parked-up in a built-up area.

ALCOHOL AND THE ROAD USER

As you become a more experienced road-user, like me, you will find that a large intake of alcohol enhances your driving skills, probly. If you're worried about the breathalyser, though, stick to that non-alcoholic lager, Heineken.

HAZARDS

The biggest hazard to driving is the police. However, if you follow the procedure shown in these diagrams, they need not be such a problem.

1 Stop!

2 All right, sunbeam, out of the motor. You're nicked.

3 Thank you very much, sir. That'll do nicely. On your way.

1

2

3

TAKING OVER

The single most important weapon in the motorist's arsenal is a proper over-taking technique. Always remember the procedure:

1 HORN, FLASHING HEADLIGHTS.
2 HORN AGAIN.
3 HORN AND LIGHTS TOGETHER.
4 SWERVE OUT WITHOUT WARNING. WANKING GESTURE OUT OF WINDOW.

At 50 mph

At 90 mph

At 130 mph

The above diagrams illustrate the number of cars you'll be able to shunt after smashing into them at the indicated speeds.

ROAD SIGNS

Some wanker who can't hold his drink

The same bloke attemping a shag

I won't go into what this one is as me Mum'll be reading this

You are requested to urinate on this sign

Increase speed now

No one over 30 allowed to drive round here

WAARGH!

Head for that puddle! Queue at bus stop

Reminder: up your quote on the car phone

Eddie Kidd

Lance taking his 3,000th Driving Test

Chance to play chicken with a choo-choo

No

Bollocks

Shut your mouth!

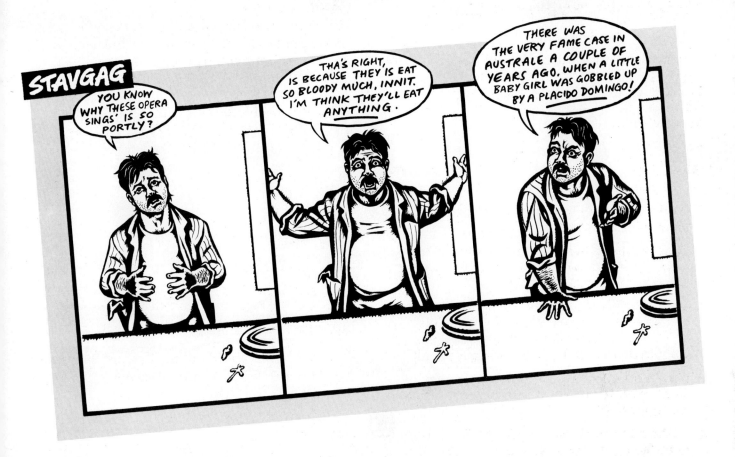

Leg it, kids,
I'm coming through

?

Aquaduct

One of them
upside down
bridges with the
river on top, it's
called a viaduct

TRAFFIC LIGHTS

RED

GO

RED
&
AMBER

GO

GREEN

GO

AMBER

GO

Prepare missile
sights

500 pts

750 pts

1,000 pts

Loadsapoints

MOTORWAY SIGNS

These are them blue, blurry things you see out of the corner of your eye on motorways. They're only there so as those wankers in the slow lane have got something to look at.

I've never seen one meself, on behalf of the truly astounding speed at which I drive, but I think they look like this, probly.

MI
THE NORTH
BUGGERALLMONEY 225
COALS-IN-BATH 240
INBREEDING 265.

SAVE THE KEBAB!

Produced by the 'Kebab Protection Society'

How much attention is afforded the humble kebab in these conservation-conscious days? Precious little, we fear. Whereas hours of television-documentary space is devoted to the plight of certain endangered species, the unfashionable kebab is ignored in favour of more glamorous animals, such as the whale and the seal. And yet its need is just as great. The kebab, considered by many to be a great delicacy, has been hunted to near extinction in its native Bethnal Green. This shy, nocturnal creature, rearely seen before 11.15 p.m., is completely at the mercy of the ruthless modern poacher with all today's technology at his fingertips. The men who practise this grisly trade are unrepentant and have even been known to snatch fledglings from the nest.

Man is the only natural enemy of the kebab and, ironically, its only chance of salvation. We urge you, therefore, to give generously to this worthy cause. Together we can stop the wholesale slaughter of kebabs on Britain's streets.

We are often told that Britain is a nation of animal lovers, so let's show the world that we care, and unite in our chosen aim to save one of the world's most endearing creatures from extinction.

The Wild kebab

HRH The Duke of Edinburgh, President of the Kebab Protection Society shooting one.

SAVE THE KEBAB!

If you wish to join our campaign, fill in the questionnaire below and send it to the address shown.

I WISH TO BECOME A FRIEND OF THE KEBAB.

MY NAME IS ....

I ENCLOSE £25 CASH.

I AM OVER TWENTY-ONE AND COMPLETELY GULLIBLE.

Please send all donations to:
Loadsamoney Enterprises Inc.
Loadsamoney House
Hackney

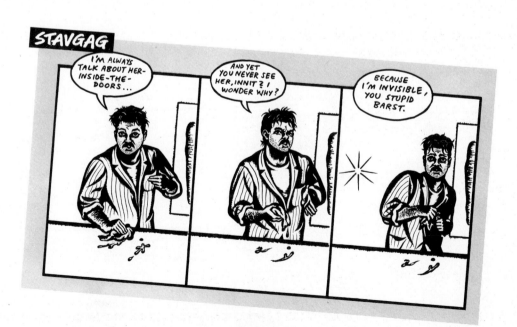

THE COUNTRY DIARY OF LOADSAMONEY

A few years ago this book come out, 'The Country Diary of Edward Wotsisname.' I never read it meself, but I'm told it sold Loadsacopies and made someone a few bob. And all it was, was just some old fashioned bird wandering about in the countryside and writing it all down. Piece of piss. I thought to meself 'I could do that.' So I've unleashed the old TNB, bosh bosh bosh, shoom shoom shoom, and here I am.

My Wad
(waddus giganticus)

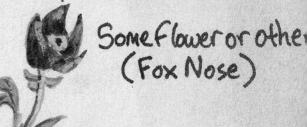

Some Flower or other
(Fox Nose)

Jan.1. (Actually it's the middle of August, but I'm not sure if you're allowed to start a diary then.) So---Trees, grass, flowers, meadows, dales... Horrible! What a load of old bollocks the countryside is, it's just one vast outside bog. Er, that's about it, really. How can you write an entire book about this dump? There's nothing here - no discos - nothing! Still, that Edward bird obviously had the same problem, 'cos she padded out her book with all, like, stupid little poems, and that. So here's one of me own ---

Cannus
Cokus

Ash
(common)

September now is come to pass,
stick some rhubarb up your arse

Jan. 2. I've had to send Lady home. My Lady, that is, not that Edward Lady. Yeah, well she only went and savaged-up an whole flock of cows, didn't she? I tried to tell the shepherd she was only playing, but he was well pissed off, miserable sod. Er, well I think I've just about covered everything about the countryside now. Am going down the pub.

Jan.3. This pub aint too bad, as it goes, nice barmaid, intelligent girl, I've christened her 'Melons'. She loves it! I reckon she's after a portion, probly. Played shove-wad with a couple of village idiots, no contest really. They only had halfpennies. Saw another cow earlier, out the window....

Hens   Moor Hens

Moor
Bleeding
Hens!

It was one of them ones with all that, like, white fluffy skin. Just stood there eating grass and goin' 'baa' for two hours! I timed it. I mean, how do you get a book out of that? Cows, eh? boring wankers, or what? Ah well, time for another crate.

'Paper is made out of trees.' Bollocks! trees are all brown and wrinkly, and paper's flat and white. Therefore - vis-a-vis, trees are made out of wood, and paper's made out of paper.

Night Jar
Sickamore

Buttock Up.

Jan 4.   Hello diary it's me again, Loadsamoney. The bloke who put the 'tree' in country. Out and about today. Yeah, I mean I didn't come down here to sit on me arse in the pub all day, did I? Not least because they're not open all day. No! I'm here to learn, expand up me knowledge and that, soak up the rural atmosphere. So i've gone down the abattoir this morning. Blinding! I wouldn't mind one of them guns -wallop!- steel bolt through the skull! Be handy for getting Lance up in the mornings. Anyway, it's fired me up with the old hunting spirit, I'm off fishing tomorrow. Got meself a detonator, and half a ton of gelagnite for bait. Should catch a couple of spratts with that little set-up!

On the tree sat a green woodpecker
So I cut it down with my Black & Decker

Dead Bird - Hit by Motor.
(Birdus Stiffus)

Tit
(Lance)

Jan 5.   Bit of a problem with the fishing. What's left of the pub's now where the Post Office used to be, and the village shop's gone into orbit. Still, the place needed livening up a bit. Lucky I came down, really. Anyway, i've had me fill of the country, so i'm going home to get this book published up before someone nicks my idea. I'm already planning a sequel, as it goes, 'Confessions of an Edwardy Bird with Big Knockers.' Should make me a fortune. I mean, i'm the bollocks at this writing game, as with everything else I put my hand to. It just comes natural to me, on behalf of I'm quite tasty at, you know, like, wording things up into good sentences and that. Yeah, I reckon I'll win Loads of Oscars for me writing these books. And another thing, my nob is, hang about, oh shit, me pen's runni-

CLASSIC COMICS PRESENT...

THE ILIAD

BY HOMER—PART 23.

FOR TEN LONG YEARS THE GREEK ARMY HAS LAIN SIEGE TO THE CITY OF TROY...

ONCE AGAIN THE GREEKS ARE REPULSED, AND THE WEARY MEN RETURN TO CAMP...

NOBLE AJAX VOICES THE THOUGHTS OF MANY GREEKS.

Christ, I'm shagged. I could murder a pint of lager...

BRAVE ACHILLES AGREES...

Yeah. And I'm bloody starving and all.

LUCKILY, HELP IS AT HAND...

Large doner please

STAV'S KEBABS
ARMY CATERING

Hello ancient peeps. How's it goin'? Rescued Her-inside-the-walls yet?

THE ARSE

RED-HAIRED ODYSSEUS DESPAIRS...

Will this war never end? Ten long years and still Troy stands. mmm - this kebab is good.

STOUT STAVROS IS THE NEXT TO SPEAK.

I'm got a blinkin' top nosh idea. Why don't you build a large gift for the Troje' peeps and hide inside it, innit?

KING MENELAUS APPLAUDS THE PLAN

It's so stupid It just might work!

90

WORK BEGINS ON THE MIGHTY STRUCTURE...

THIS IS A HARD HAT AREA!!

STAVROS IS TIRELESS IN DIRECTING THE WORK

A little more salad on top... not too much onion... careful with those chips.

AND AT LAST THE WORK IS FINISHED.

A giant wooden kebab!

Surely it was supposed to be a horse.

Shut up you daft git.

HOMER RECORDS THAT THE STUPID BLOODY TROJANS FELL FOR IT.

Look - an enormous kebab. It must be a gift from the Greeks.

Yum yum - open the gates.

Hooray - I hope there's plenty of chilli sauce - slurp!

INSIDE THE KEBAB...

Ho ho! I think this kebab is gonna be too hot even for the Trojans.

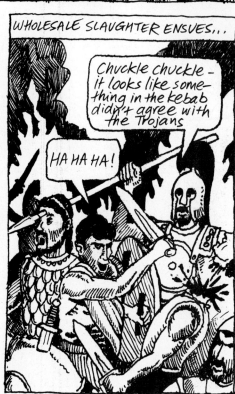

WHOLESALE SLAUGHTER ENSUES...

Chuckle chuckle - it looks like something in the kebab didn't agree with the Trojans

HA HA HA!

GOD BLESS MUNNY

MUNY IS SUMTHING THAT GROWN UPS MAKE TOGETHER
WEN THE CHILDREN HAVE GONE TOO SLEEP

Sarah, age 7

munny ie the most
important thing in the
world because if people
did not have munny
they would be poor

Lyn, age 8

munny means never
having to say you
are sorry

Michael, age 11

If I had lots of
munny I would hire
a hit man to kill
my sister.

Rory, age 9

munny means That when
your hamster dies you
can just go out and get
another one

Amanda, age 8

my granny gives me ten pee
when she comes out of the
geriatric ward for the day
I say "10 pee? give us a pound
you senile old miser."

Glenn, age 9

there's more to life than munny - there's LoadsaMunny

Nigel, chancellor of the exchequer, age 147½

BUGGERALL'S HORRORSCOPES

Your Stars by Buggerallmoney

CANCER
Y' gonna meet a shoart, dark, veealent stranger smerkin' tabs who'll bring a fist into conjonction wi'yowwah nots.

VIRGO
Travel will feature highly for ye in the next two days. Yees'll be gannin' through a bloody windoah, pal.

SCORPIO
Uranus will be on the cusp o' yowwah feeyus by the time ah've finished with ye, pal.

CAPRICORN
Noah mattah how bad things may appeah to be at the merment, they're ganna getta lot bloody worse by the middle o' next week, which is what ah'm gonna knock ye intah.

PISCES
Divven ye worry about yowwah stars, ye'll be seein' plenty o' them the dee, pal.

ARIES
Who are yees lookin' at?

GEMINI
Ye'll shoartly meet some o' yowwah departed relatives.

LEO
Yower deed as well, pal.

LIBRA
And ye.

AQUARIUS
And ye tee

SAGITTARIUS
Reet, owtside! The lorra yas.

TAURUS
Yower, greeyut, yower. Todeeyah will bring ye plenty o' tabs and beeyah, and the oppahtunity to ponch a lorra people who aren't yow.

FAMOUS TAUREANS
Buggerallmoney.

Sometimes when all the presh' of life is get up you' nerve-endings and on you' nose, a chap is need to do something to relax, as Frankie Goes to Howerd is say. And my fave form of relax' is to go clubbin'.

To go out clubbin' you got to dress right. So, in the words of the old Cole Port' song:

I'm pullin' on me plus fours,
Stickin' on me check cap,
Tyin' up me spats!

Tha's right, golf, the sport of badly dressed peeps all round the world. Simply whip out you' Mashie Niblik, and all the cares of the globe is just fade away. Ah, yes, the beautifully tend' greens, the glorious fairways, a bit of rough in the bunk-up with your four iron.

There is many great courses in the Brish Islands – Troon, St Andrews, Aintree – but the greatest of them all, as far as I'm concern', is, of course, Bournemouth! I mean, all those other courses is bloody boring or what, innit? Is just a lot of grass and bloody miles between the holes, blimey, you is spend half you time walking about. But in Bourn' they is got windmills, see-saws, castles, old bits of drain pipe and, of course, the famous seventh hole, the clown's trousers.

Is a magnif' course, eleven holes. It used to be nine, but a couple of rabbits is escape from the nearby kiddies' zoo and burrow out two excitin' new holes, which are the envy of many more fame' golf courses.

Yes, for me the golf is much more than just a hobby-horse, is a blinkin' obsesh'. I'm remember a great round last year. It was a lovely crisp morn, a light mist is lay across the wiggly S-bend. I'm three below par, with a birdie on the sixth, it was a herring-gull, I'm think. But anyway, I'm shoo it away and prepare to tea off. This is where a good caddy is come in very useful, and Her Inside the Doors is one of the best. 'How many shoogs you want, Stav?' she is say, and I'm say, 'FORE!' and let fly with my trusty wood. Is a perfect shot, is rocket away at about a thousand mile an hour, and is smack straight into the side of the parkie's hut, bounce off, rebound off a passin' old age pensh' and is caught in the air by the herring-gull who is drop it straight down the hole.

'Hole in one!' I'm shout jubilantly.

'No, they is all right,' says Her Inside the Doors, studyin' the teabags.

At this point, the enraged parkie is come out of his hut blindin' and effin'. Luckily, Her Inside the Doors is equal to the situashe'. She is calmy select a putter and is explain to him that if he's not bugger off, she's goin' to stick it where the sun he does not shine.

So I'm able to continue my game in peace. I'm eventch' went round in 378, a new course record, and I'm greatly improve my handclap. I'm reck' if I keep on like this, I'm shortly get a call from American Express, askin' me to do their next ad. Because, let's face it, you can't understan' a blimmin' word that Stefi Bollocksteros is say.

I'm already work out my speech: 'Do you know me? Tha's right, Stavros Dukakis. Are we nearly full yet? Blimey, I'm better put the other one in, innit? Don' worry, I'm ride it home.'

Yes, golf is mean a great deal to me. Is not just ploddin' about the countrysides all day hittin' a little ball in a stupid hole. There's much more to it than that. The old-age tradishe', the camera-ra-derie, the sound of leather on willow an' those bloody great big multi-coloured umbrollies. Her Inside the Doors is pick one up for me from the garden of the Butcher's Arms one night. Which brings me to the main attracsh' of golf, the nineteenth, or waterin' hole (as we call it in golfin' circulars). Here you can wine away the long summer eves gettin' on the wrong side of a bottle of brand' an' swap tall stories about the one tha's get away.

In the crazy-golf club house at Bournemouth you is often rub shoulds with golfin' celebs like Brute Forsyth-Saga, little Ronnie the Corbs and even Dennis 'the Menace' Thatch', who is sometimes come down to escape from Her Inside the Cabinet, innit?

What a merry band of drunken old codgers we all is.

Peeps is often ask me how I'm would like to drop dead in an ideal world. And I'm say, 'I would like to pop my cork on the golf course at Bourn', scorin' a hole in one an' watchin' the Arse beat Spurs.' Then I could stroll up that fairway to Heaven, a happy old Stav.

I'm couldn't get Her-Inside-The-Doors to pose for this pic so I'm got my cuz George to cad'.

STAV'S GOLFING PAGE

94

·BOB SAYS PLEASE· DON'T HIT ME AGAIN,' BUGGERALLMONEY!

Aye reet. Well it all storted, reet, when I sees this dorty greet perster behind this blerk's head that I'm hittin' sayin' 'Auditions fa BBC Talent Contest'. I says to meself, 'Talent contest! Tharral be ta see who can doon tha merst beers. I'm on forrit!' So I'm ganninn along and they puts me in this room wirra neen ya oold lass, and ah've gan, 'hoo there! I'm alreet here! I can drink her oonder tha teeble!' and then some puff wirra clipboard anna stopwatch roond his neck cooms in and I says te him, 'Where's tha beers, bastad? and he says, 'I'm sorry, ye've coome in tha wrong pleeyus. Next!' So I'm gannin, 'I'll sher yee wots next, pal,' and I left his stopwatch soomwer up be hes kidnees. Then I'm gannin inte th' next room lookin' te help meself, leek and there's this dorty greet fat blerk sittin' up the end drinkin shumpeeun and smerkin' a tab thru a gerly herlder and he says, 'Wot d'ye do?' Well, I'm gannin', 'I drink beer and smerk tabs,' and he's gannin', 'Wull tharrint mooch of an act. D'ya dee owt else?' I'm gannin', 'Ay, I poonch people inna mooth. Espeshly fat Soothun bastards drinkin' shumpeeun and smerkin' tabs thru' a gerly herlder.' and he's gannin', 'A, well, that's queet different. Tha soonds juss tha sorra act we're lookin' for.' and I'm gannin', 'Ya not juss sayin' tha sos I

wern't poonch ya, are yees?' and he's gannin', 'Ner, abslootly not.' and I'm gannin', 'Ah, wull that's alreet then,' and I redeccareeuts the room wuth hes breeuns, leek. Then this utha blerk wot's heedin' oonder the teeble ses, 'De ya have an eagint orr de ya looks after yersell?' I ses, 'I can look after mesell – look, pal!' Ay, that were his testicles tellt. Wull, it terns oot I've gorra go doon te London and appear on telly. So I gets on the boos te tha Worr Memorrial, and after a birra thumpin' the boos dreever agrees te teak me doon that BBC Telly Cen'a. Well, I gets doon that 'Bob Says' office, and thes blerk ses, 'I've come te teak ya te meeacoop.' Wull, that were him deed fa stortas. Than thes lass ses dee i wanna wearra soote sos as te cree-eut a gud impreshun. I ses, 'I divven dee impreshuns, luv, i drink beer, now were the frigg is it?' Ser thus blerk papes oop and ses, 'Wud ye lake me te sher ye the wee te horspitallity?' I ses, 'Ernly won of os es gurin te horspital, pal, and tha's yee!' and I pollished tha peevmunt wi' hes feeuse. So I'm gannin' doon tha bar, and I'm joos gerrin Syd Little te lend us a fiver befoor I tred on his glasses whan the lass wot thert I did impreshuns cooms oop and ses she's bin sent te keep tabs on me. I ses, 'Bloody greeut! I'll huv ferty Reegul and I'll smerk tha lorrin tha lift.' Wull, she

teaks us te tha steurdieur and thurs a cooppul a oothar acts hungin' aboot ootseede. Well, wun of 'em ses, 'Wudda yees dee?' I ses, 'Worrasit gorra dee wuth yee, bastard? Ye moost be teo borrals shert ovva picnic!' Wull, he ses, 'Nah, mon, I'm aal singin', aal dancin', aal roond fumilee un-erteenar.' So afta gevvin 'im a birra attenshun I'm gannin', 'Seems te me yorraal bits and peeuses, aal ooer the flawer, pal.' Than this ootha blerk ses, 'I'm a stund-oop comic.' So I poonch the bastard te tha fleer and ses, 'Worraye deein' layin doon thun?' Than I'm gannin' te thes oother tertal bastard, 'Worra yees dee?' and he's gannin', 'I'm a mjishun, I pull hunkercheefs oota peeple's eears.' I ses, 'Tha's nowt! I can pull eears off the seed a peeples heeds – look! and lastly thur was thes puff wot sed he cud bend spoons joos bay tha fowace o' hes personality, ser I yersed tha fowace o' ma personality te bend hes legs roond tha back o' hes neck. Wull I were reet pesst off te see tharra lorra acts storted te seay aboot noo tha' they reconed they wudden botha gooin on afta orl, boot than 'Bob Ses' himsell coomes oot & tulls 'em thurs ner reesun te be noavuss. I ses, 'I'll give ye summit te be noavuss aboot!' and I weeped tha smeel off hes feeus and purrit roond tha buck o' hes

boertie. Unnyweers, tha sher storts and tha ferst act on is the neen yor aal lass, hoo storts tellin' th' ordience that the steeuge es en hor blood. Wull, I gers on and meeuks it tha ootha wee roond. Than tiw oother lasses coom on and stort worblin' 'Tha poowa o' loove', burrit were morra ceeus o' 'Tha poowa o' electrisitty' whun I reweered tha meecrapherns and sent feeve thoosand verlts doon ther larynx. Feenalee Bob say'a, 'Wulcerm Buggerallmoney' frum tha seeufty o' hes dressin rum, and I gers on and telt the ooerdience tha' me act was a threrbuck te simple erldfashund vareeity. 'Worram gonna dee is pick a blerk at randerm from yees lot nd I'm gonna poonch the shite oota hem and I'm gonna carry oon poonchin' that shite oota tha lorrayes oontil I win!' Wull, I'd hordly storted me act on a penshuner frum Ceeutterum whun the ooerdience verted uz the winnah! Norrooernly did I get tha merst apploerse, burraal tha ootha acts coom on and apploerded me as wull!

I'm gannin in fa *Neur Feeuses 89* next. I rorther funcy huvvin' a goer at geein' thut Marty Ceeune 89 neur feeuses. Boot in tha meentaime, as Bob ses, 'If opperteaunity cooms yao weeah . . . knock tha bastads heed off!'